other stories

PAPER BASTION
and
other stories

Meera Kant

Translated from Hindi by
Ranjana Kaul

Rupa . Co

Published 2011 by
Rupa Publications India Pvt. Ltd.
7/16, Ansari Road, Daryaganj,
New Delhi 110 002

Sales Centres:

Allahabad Bengaluru Chennai
Hyderabad Jaipur Kathmandu
Kolkata Mumbai

Printed in India by
Nutech Photolithographers
B-240, Okhla Industrial Area, Phase-I,
New Delhi 110 020

To my beacon
Dr Sushma Bhatnagar

Contents

The Bride's Alley

Often lanes and alleys are famous for their names or, at times, infamous for reasons good or bad. But when unnamed lanes acquire a name, their silent namelessness is wiped out from the minds of people, like a street despoiled at midnight by the body of a dog crushed under the wheels of a vehicle, is swept clean and spotless by sweepers in the morning.

The day Nagina married Razzak and came to the middle house in this blind alley of three houses in the butchers' cluster of Kasabpura, no one could have imagined that this nameless alley would acquire a name so soon.

Razzak Qureshi was an orphan; the only person he could call his own was his elder brother Ramzani. Their parents had left nothing for them except the house in the butchers' cluster, which had a room and a courtyard with another small room on the first floor and an open terrace. The boys had not got along with each other since childhood, and there was no possibility of it happening now. Ramzani had occupied the room and terrace upstairs as soon as he got married because it had a door which could be shut when required. The ground floor had three walls and a tarpaulin could be hung in front to give it the semblance of a room. This three-walled room had an alcove in which household stuff could be stored as and when it was acquired. There was also a similar three-walled kitchen in the courtyard. The stairs to Ramzani's room did not go up from the courtyard but from the outside, so after his wedding there was no interaction between the couple and Razzak. Yes, sometimes while going up and down the stairs Ramzani would lean over to look into the courtyard.

For two years, that is while Ramzani's wife was there, every evening such a shower of loud abuses and foul language would unleash that all the residents of the alley were forced to sit with their fingers stuffed inside their ears. Soon Ramzani's wife stopped cursing him and quietly eloped with Jugnu, the vegetable-seller.

Due to Ramzani's intemperance and Razzak's quick temper, the two brothers were not even on speaking terms with each other. Their lives, like their homes, were totally separate. To the extent that when Ramzani was looking for his wife and frequenting the police station in search of news about her, Razzak, who knew the truth, did not inform him that Jugnu was the culprit.

Ramzani did attend Razzak's wedding wearing a new *tehmad* but he was invited, like everyone else in the alley, by the barber, not by his brother. All the men of the cluster participated in the wedding procession and all the residents of the alley relished a feast of roti and *korma* to celebrate the arrival of the bride. Not a single person stayed home. The children attacked the sweet *pulao* like crows swooping down on offal.

For a few days the older women, who had welcomed Nagina on her arrival in that single-room house, performed their duty as elders and landed up at her house early morning every day with a fold of *paan* in their mouths. They would sit there on a string cot till the evening, chopping betel nuts into thin slices and chatting about the daily affairs. At midday they would go back in groups of two's and three's with their white burqas over their heads and return in an hour or so. In the evening, before Razzak's return, they would go back leaving her with blessings and good wishes. For them Nagina was the 'Dulhan', the bride. So every morning they would call out to each other from their windows, roofs or the alley, 'O, Bi, aren't you coming?'

'Where?'

'Where else! The bride's house.'

Nagina was called 'Dulhan' by everyone in the cluster. Like the others, even she forgot her real name. No one remembered how and who called that narrow, nameless alley the 'Bride's alley' for the first time, but that was how it came to be known by everyone gradually.

A few months later the bride's brother came unannounced in the middle of the afternoon one day. That day only two old ladies had come over to the Dulhan's house and they too had gone back to eat their lunch. When she heard what her brother said Dulhan did not even wait for the old ladies, she just locked the front door and left for her parents' home with her brother. On the way the brother handed over the key of the house to a friend of his and told him to give it to Razzak.

The bride was quite certain that she would return before dark, but she nevertheless sent the key to Razzak as a precaution. However, she could not return that night, and for many more nights. When she finally came back on a Tuesday, the abattoir was closed and Razzak was at home.

It was nine o'clock in the morning. Her heart was beating wildly as she stepped into the alley. She had gone without telling Razzak. Who knew what would happen? She crossed the first house and then paused momentarily at the door of the second house. It was fully open. There was a dirty jute curtain hanging at the door whose lower edge had become ragged and uneven with the passage of time. Pushing the curtain aside, she entered the courtyard and saw Razzak making tea on the coal stove. It seemed that he had just woken up. She took her burqa off quickly, saying, 'Are you making tea? Move aside, I will do it.'

Razzak didn't pay any attention. She hung her burqa on a peg in the wall and came near him, 'Come on, let me make it.' Razzak stood up. He pulled her plait so hard that her chin was pushed upwards, 'So you met your mother's new husband?' The bride moaned in pain. He dragged her by the hair into the room and threw her with such force on the cot that her head swam after ramming into one of its legs. Razzak climbed onto the cot saying, 'Don't ever imagine that you can also find another husband and I will just walk around adjusting my *tehmad* knot like your wimp of a father.' The bride was unconscious.

When she recovered after a while she heard her own whimper. Suddenly she realised her legs were bare. Supporting her head with her hands she sat up with a jerk and folded her legs. Her salwar was lying on the ground. She felt some wetness around her thighs. The whole house smelt as though something was burning. When she peeped into the courtyard she found the tea had boiled dry on the stove. The door was shut; she was alone in the house. When she tried to open the door, she found it closed from outside.

She sat down on the floor. As she touched her head gingerly, she let out a sharp cry, 'Oh, mother!' She remembered Ammi, her mother, once again. Only God knew where she had gone with her new husband! It was good that Abba, her father, had left the butchers' cluster many years ago with his family and gone to settle in Mangolpuri. Otherwise all the residents of the cluster would be discussing her mother's disgrace now. Suddenly the bride was struck by a thought. How did Razzak come to know about it? If Razzak knows, everyone in the butchers' cluster must be having this news. Anyway whatever has to happen, will happen. After all it is not me, but my mother who has run off with another man. The whore! She must be enjoying herself while Abba has been left behind to look after four children. It is good that I am already married. Otherwise I would also have become a burden for Abba. God knows where she is, the shameless hussy!

The bride mentally cursed her mother. She used all the swear words she knew but somehow they seemed to lack any fire or severity. There was a corner of her being where a waterfall seemed to have burst forth because of this incident, and perhaps its drops were falling on the fire and cooling it down.

As Dulhan uttered the word 'shameless', she visualised the barefoot seven-year-old girl herding goats in the village of Akbarganj near Raibareilly, a girl whom she hadn't seen at that young age but whom she had heard about. This girl was Katori whom Nagina had addressed as 'Ammi' till now. How much Ammi has suffered since her childhood! All her life she has lived by the dictates of others. First grandfather, then father, and then her husband! Why is the society so pained if she is following the dictates of her own heart for the first time? Where was this pain when for months the seven-year-old child was trying to run away from starvation, from the terrifying hunger which followed her with its wild streaming hair and large teeth calling out to her, 'Katori, Katori...'

Ammi used to say that one year it rained so hard in Raibareilly that all the villages were flooded. Everything was destroyed; everything that was saved up was washed away. The crops were destroyed. There was no grain left at all, just famine everywhere. Then the news came that the government was distributing rations to flood-affected villagers in some far-off place. Katori's grandfather called his four sons and decided that their wives would also accompany them to collect the rations. So, the women who had never left the confines of the village now set out with drums and tins to follow their husbands. There was one bicycle in the house. Some tins were tied to it as well using tyre strips. The villagers had assumed that all their drums and tins would be filled with wheat and rice but they found that only a certain quantity of grain was being distributed according to the number of family members. When they returned home, grandfather once again called all the sons and their wives and announced that henceforth only the men and the boys in the family would be given rice and rotis. The women would eat the leftovers and drink rice gruel. The girls in the family would get some roasted mix made from parched gram and *Mahua* flowers. Ma had said that even if one of the boys left some rotis or if one of them was away, his portion would be kept in the baskets suspended from the roof so that the girls could not steal it.

After doing all the household chores, the seven-year-old Katori would only get the dry gram mixture to curb her hunger and she would chew it for hours swallowing it with the spit in her mouth.

The flood actually broke the back of Katori's family. After a few years her sister and then Katori were married off. At that time Katori was merely thirteen years old and her husband was around thirty-five. When Katori came to the butchers' cluster in Delhi after her marriage she found that her husband already had three children, all of whom were older to her. There was also a fifty-year-old mother-in-law. She got enough food to fill her stomach after doing backbreaking work the whole day but she also had to bear the slaps and blows of her husband.

Dulhan had witnessed all this with her own eyes. One evening her mother's lip had split so badly that it didn't stop bleeding for hours despite the salve they put on it. After Abba left for work she had accompanied her mother to Irwin hospital where the doctor had put two stitches on her lip. What was wrong if she ran away from such a hell?

The bride was lost in these thoughts when the door opened and Razzak entered the house. Seeing her sitting on the floor he lost his temper and hit her with one booted foot, 'Daughter of a whore! Sitting there without a salwar…just the way I left you, are you waiting for Ramzani with your bare legs wide open? Waiting till he sees you as he climbs up the stairs?'

The bride could say nothing except a pain-filled 'Allah'. She somehow managed to gain some coherence and moved towards the cot. She was just picking up her salwar when Razzak who was sitting on his haunches lighting a *beedi*, remarked in a conversational tone, 'By the way, what was your mother thinking? Didn't the old man feed her?' The bride didn't answer and started slipping her right leg into the salwar while sitting on the cot.

'*Arre*, has your shameless mother taken your tongue away with her? Why don't you answer?'

The bride put her second leg into the salwar. 'Obstinate woman! Are you going to answer me, or should I get up again and break your arms and legs?'

Holding the drawstring of her salwar Dulhan suddenly shouted, 'He was a butcher…a butcher like you, that is why…'

Razzak lost his mind completely; he grabbed the bride by her shoulder and stubbed his *beedi* out on her waist.

'Oh mother!' Dulhan writhed in pain.

Days and nights slowly slipped by, as she dealt with her backache along with a life as listless as death. Her house would no longer be filled with the crowd of older women from the neighbourhood. The thin line denoting the bride's alley, despite being the most recently demarcated, had been erased from the map of the butchers' cluster of Kasabpura which they carried in their minds. Once or twice she had gathered courage, worn a burqa and gone to visit them. But they asked her so many questions about her mother that she felt much more comfortable in her own house surrounded by walls which seemed to be painted with boredom, days which dozed in laziness and hunchbacked evenings which moved slowly and painfully. She would put the griddle on fire as soon as Razzak returned home in the evening and offer him fresh warm rotis with meat and onions. Razzak would come to life as soon as he had eaten and he would become so impatient that he would drag her towards the cot without even letting her tidy the kitchen.

'What are you doing…at least let me put out the fire.'

'Leave the fire, help me cool down first.' The bride would tremble in apprehension.

One day she asked him shyly, 'Do you love me so much?'

'Go on! What are you saying . . .?'

'Then what?' the bride's eyes asked, filled with languor.

'It has just become a habit,' Razzak replied setting her arm with the enamel bangles behind her back.

'Like swearing and using foul language?'

Razzak did not have time to listen to what she was saying. So, he did not consider it necessary to answer her. He just went on doing what he liked.

Mournful music being played on some instrument coming from the blind end of the bride's alley gradually filtered into her house.

'Who plays this music?' she asked, heaving a tired sigh.

'How does it concern you? Mind your own business. I will break your teeth if you start looking around, understand?' Razzak wiped his sweat and, lying on his back, looked up at the rings in the ceiling.

The bride stopped asking any questions but she felt some affinity with the music. Every evening she would wait for it as though she was waiting for some news from her home or the arrival of someone dear to her.

Turning over, Razzak pulled her close again.

'Be patient,' Dulhan blurted.

'Do I come home hungry and tired after a hard day's work just to be patient?' Razzak was already on top of her. She only managed to heave a sigh. She cursed him in her mind. What kind of a butcher is he? Even a butcher wipes his blade clean before the second kill. He takes the name of Allah. But this scoundrel doesn't even give a chance to take a deep breath. Just one kill after another... after another... after another . . .

The bride got up after a while when she heard Razzak snoring. She felt sick when she touched her body which felt like a dirty knife had been used to butcher something. Wrapping Razzak's dirty *tehmad* around her, she walked out to have a bath in the middle of the night.

After God knows how many tired mornings, stale afternoons yawning with boredom and panting nights, one day Razzak came back from the abbatoir with a tiny six-day-old goat kid bleating with hunger.

'Here, take care of this baby goat, it is hungry,' Razzak said, as he put the kid down. When the bride stroked the goat's back affectionately, it trembled; a tremor which travelled straight along the bride's arm to her heart.

'Get a nipple tomorrow, we will feed it with a milk bottle,' Dulhan said as she fetched a small ball of cotton wool. Then she and Razzak fed the baby goat, taking turns to squeeze some milk from the cotton wool into its mouth. She watched Razzak as he lifted his arm trying to put some milk into the goat's raised mouth. For the first time she felt some affection for him, she wanted to shower him with her love.

'We will look after it,' she said in a soft voice.

'It is not your plaything...what did you think? We will fatten it up so that we can get a good price for it.'

'What?' the bride asked in surprise, 'Are you going to sell it?'

'No,' Razzak replied dropping the ball of cotton wool in the bowl, 'I will cook it on your wedding.' Then he shouted, swearing at her, 'Get up! I want my food.'

The bride was a little heart-broken but such disappointments were so much a part of her daily life that she did not even pause to think about them any longer.

'We will call it Bhuri,' she said, stroking the brown patches on the goat's white hide and then moved towards the stove.

Bhuri became a part of her life. The bride would be busy with it the whole day. She would feed it in the afternoon and then, tying it up outside the door, she would close the door and take a nap. One day someone knocked at the door in the afternoon. Had Razzak come home early? She was surprised. No, if it had been Razzak he would have banged at the door and his foul language would have woken up the entire neighbourhood. Then who? She got up and called out loudly standing near the door, 'Who is it?'

'It is me, Gauri…mother says please move your goat away. It is dirtying our doorstep.' She opened the door on hearing the voice; it was the six or seven-year-old girl who lived in the first house in the alley. The bride had seen her and her mother a few times but they had not talked to each other in the past few months.

'It dirties the place?' the bride asked playfully.

'Yes, come out and see. We are expecting guests this evening.'

The bride smiled. She came out adjusting the dupatta on her head and pulled Bhuri inside. Then she came back with a broom and swept all the goat droppings from the alley and threw them in the gutter. As she was returning with her broom she saw Gauri at the door of her house.

'This is not a goat,' she said.

'Then…?' Gauri asked in surprise.

'Bhuri…it is brown…just like you are *gori*, fair.'

'But I am not *gori*.'

'So are you black?'

'No, I am Gauri.' The child shrugged her shoulder and went inside her house. The bride also entered her own house pushing aside the jute curtain on the door with a smile on her face.

The next day Dulhan kept listening for any sounds outside her door. As soon as she heard a soft thud on the door of the first house in the alley, she peeped out from the curtain. It was Gauri.

'Hey, Gauri!' Gauri turned back when the bride called out, 'Have your guests left?'

'Yes, my mama had come. He brought a new frock for me.' Gauri ran her hands on the frock she was wearing.

'Oh, it is really lovely. Listen, who else is there in your house?'

'My mother, father, I and my brother.'

'How old is your brother?'

'Very old. He is studying in the tenth class.'

'Who is in the house right now?'

'Ma, who else?'

'And your...your papa?'

'Papa goes to the office.'

'Is your mother sleeping?'

'No, she is chopping some fenugreek.'

Dulhan stepped out of her door and walked across to Gauri's house. The door was open. Gauri's mother was sitting on a wooden plank in the courtyard and was busy cleaning fenugreek. Dulhan sat down on the wide stone doorsill.

'Oh, come in, come in...come inside,' Gauri's mother said.

'I am fine here, I can keep an eye on my own door from here.'

'I just saw you the first day when you came as a bride! I came with Aneesa's mother,' Gauri's mother said.

'Yes, when she gave me your gift she mentioned that you also lived in this alley.'

'But I never saw you again after that.'

'Yes, my husband...' Dulhan stopped in the middle of her sentence.

'He is very bad tempered,' Gauri's mother completed it for her. 'These men, they are always ready to lose their temper.'

Dulhan smiled as she adjusted the dupatta on her head.

'*Arre*, come over sometimes in the afternoon. The men are not around at that time and there is no one except the two of us in the alley.' Gauri's mother's lack of formality increased the bride's confidence.

'There is another house ahead, isn't there?' she asked.

'Yes, but both of them are teachers. They go to some school far away and return only in the evening. Their children also come back with them.'

'They are teachers...but then what do they play at night?'

'Oh, that! Green sahib is a Christian. He plays the hymns and songs that are sung in his church.'

Gauri's mother was giving her the answers to all those questions which Razzak would never answer. Gradually Dulhan got into the habit of going and sitting there everyday. Gauri's mother would be washing clothes or winnowing rice. The two of them would chat for hours while Gauri wrote on her slate with chalk in the courtyard or studied inside with her brother. Not only Gauri's mother but even Gauri and her brother thought of Nagina as 'Dulhan'. She could share her loneliness and pour her heart out because Gauri's mother didn't belong to her family or her community.

'Gauri's mother, you are alone just like me. At least I can hear the sounds, the voices, the quarrels from other houses around but you are not even living amidst your own people. How did you come to the butchers' cluster?'

'It's been ten years now, Gauri was even born here. *Arre*, where can you get a house on a reasonable amount in Delhi?

My husband's friend Ashfaq sahib is the one who got us this house. There is some sort of legal problem relating to the roof of the house, so we got it quite cheap. And then how does the neighbourhood matter! Once you close the door your entire world is inside.'

Dulhan remained silent and tried to understand her feelings. Gauri's mother droned on, 'It is just a matter of a few days, soon you will be expecting a child and then you will get busy with your own work.' The bride smiled, hoping her words would come true.

And then when she discovered that she really was expecting she gave the news first to Gauri's mother. 'You are the one who blessed me, so I am giving you the news first. If my own people had been close by…' Dulhan's eyes clouded with tears.

'*Arre*, those who help you in moments of pain and sorrow are the ones who are truly your own. Tell your husband and then talk to one of the elder women in the neighbourhood. Go to the doctor. If you want I will come with you to the hospital, but first check at home.'

Sitting on the doorsill of Gauri's house Dulhan was now busy knitting sweaters, caps and socks for her third child just as she had knitted them for the first two. Her elder daughter Nargis was three years old and the younger one, Mubina, was a year and three months old.

'Gauri's mother, I should better leave now. Razzak is about to come.'

'Why, is he coming home early today?'

'Yes, the abattoir is shut today, there is a strike. He has gone to sell some goats for someone, he should be back soon.' The bride gathered her wool and got up.

'So that is why you are wearing a *garara* today!' Gauri's mother remarked with a sparkle in her eyes. The bride laughed to hide her embarrassment.

'I will give you the cloth if you know how to cut a *garara*... I will stitch it myself.'

'*Arre*, are you going to wear a *garara*?'

They both burst into laughter. Then Gauri's mother controlled her laughter and explained, 'No, we only wear saris after marriage. I wanted to make one for Gauri, she is still a child but she is very keen to wear one.'

'Yes, yes, send it, I will even stitch it for you.' Dulhan walked towards her own house. Razzak had said he would buy some sweets for children from Jama Masjid and who knew he might listen to her and take them for an outing as well. She entered the house, pulled the sheet over Nargis and Mubina who were sleeping on the cot and started washing spinach. If I add it to the meat it will change the taste of the dish, she thought. She lit the coal fire and prepared the gravy for meat. Once she had finished, she swept the courtyard while waiting for Razzak. She was constantly bunching up her *garara* as she walked around. She dusted the basket in which she used to hang the leftover pieces of roti. Then she remembered something and walked towards the kitchen. She took some rotis out of the bread basket, broke them into pieces and put them in the hanging basket. She thought they would dry in the sun and then they could be used in difficult times. In the meanwhile Nargis and Mubina had woken up and taken a round of the alley. Three-year-old Nargis would often pick up Mubina, hold her against her right hip, and walk around the entire neighbourhood.

The night had descended. This was the time Razzak usually returned but he was nowhere in sight. She gave the children some rotis and some meat and spinach and started changing her clothes. Nargis was breaking the bread into pieces and eating it while Mubina licked the gravy. That day she had taken the purple *garara* with golden lace out of her trunk and worn it, hoping that Razzak would take them out seeing her all dressed up. But there was no hope. All her efforts and dreams were useless. He didn't even return home. He could swear and shout at her if he wanted but at least he should come back home. She had put in all that effort needlessly.

Just then Razzak entered the house. He handed over a packet wrapped in newspaper to the bride saying, 'Here is some meat, cook it well.'

'Is it beef?'

'Your father has gifted me the entire abattoir, hasn't he, so that I can feed you goat meat everyday?'

The girls were frightened. Nargis pushed the platter aside and shifted towards the corner. Mubina also followed her.

'Why are you getting angry? I just asked…' the bride said.

'Come on, give me my dinner.'

While Razzak was eating Dulhan picked up Mubina and started breast-feeding her. She no longer had any milk left in her body but Mubina did not sleep without sucking. Nargis had put her dish under the tap and gone to sleep pulling the sheet over herself. Dulhan pulled the sleeping Mubina away from her chest and put her to sleep with Nargis. The moon was strolling across the sky, peeping into the bride's courtyard and illuminating the room without a door.

'I wore a *garara* today, a purple one,' Dulhan said.

'Why? Did you go somewhere?'

'No, I was waiting for you,' Dulhan answered, handing him a glass of water.

Razzak turned and caught her wrist, 'Then where are you going?'

'To eat my dinner.'

'You can eat later, first come here...' Razzak pulled her towards him with such force that she fell in his lap.

'Oh! What are you doing? The children will wake up.'

'They won't wake up, they've just gone to sleep...cover their faces with the sheet.' Razzak pulled the bride down to the ground. Then who bothered about covering the children's faces! When Razzak finally got up slathered in sweat the bride gathered herself together and started to get up. Razzak held her arm, 'Stay there.'

'This is enough, think of my condition,' Dulhan said.

'What is the big deal? You are just in your fifth month,' Razzak said, stroking her stomach. 'We can wait a while if you are tired, I will smoke a *beedi*.'

He stretched out his hand, picked up the bundle of *beedis* and the matchbox from the shelf and lit his *beedi*. His hands were wandering over the bride's thighs as he smoked. Suddenly he said, 'Soft grass!' The bride was already half-asleep but his words reached her ears. When Razzak glanced at her, her eyes were shut. She is already intoxicated, he thought to himself. First she doesn't let you touch her and then she is completely lost. These women! Suddenly he thought of something, he lifted his arm and picked up the match box. Dulhan opened her eyes when she heard the sound of the match stick being lit. Was he planning to smoke another *beedi*? She was confused because he was already clenching a *beedi* in his teeth and gazing steadily at the flame of the match. He was gradually bringing it closer and closer to her thighs. She was shocked, 'Get away! What are you doing?' She tried to get up. Razzak held her left leg down tightly, 'Stay there.'

The hand with the lighted match was coming closer and closer. 'Let me go, you scoundrel, let me go!' The bride gathered all her strength and tried to free herself but Razzak just held on and pulled her leg towards him. Bringing the flaming match a little closer, he said, 'Nothing will happen to you, just let me see, I will put it out immediately.'

'Let me go...you bastard...may you rot...' Razzak's hold became stronger. The flame of the match was dancing in the pupils of his eyes. The bride felt warmth on her leg, she screamed, 'Oh God!' The scream, which was like the cry of an animal before being slaughtered, echoed through the room and the courtyard. She lifted her right leg up and smashed it into Razzak's chest. His head hit the wall and the match fell down singeing his finger. The bride jumped up. She picked up the salwar lying on the floor, opened the door of the house, and ran out into the alley. In the darkness she quickly wore her salwar, panting. Suddenly the door of the house slammed shut, 'Now stay outside, you whore!'

'Open the door, you rogue, open it.' She banged the door shouting all the obscenities she had learnt in her life. But there was complete silence inside. In the dark alley the bride leaned against the wall and sobbed. For the first time she was out in the alley without a dupatta to cover her. She spent the night wrapped in darkness, sleeping and crying, leaning her head against her knees.

It was three o'clock at night. Mubina woke up and started crying when she did not find her mother next to her. Her crying woke up Nargis who also looked around for her mother. Razzak tried to quieten them by shouting but this frightened them so much that they started crying even louder. The bride shouted from outside, '*Arre*, open the door, the children are crying.'

Nargis was crying, 'Ammi…' Razzak said, 'A djinn has taken your mother away…go to sleep, otherwise he will take you away as well.' Nargis burst into loud sobs as soon as she heard about the djinn. Razzak's sleep had already been disturbed. He got up and opened the door, 'Come in…take care of your offal. They just keep crying the entire night.' He lay down and dozed off. The bride rushed in and her daughters clung to her. She had no idea when she fell asleep holding the two girls in her arms. In the morning she was awakened by Razzak's voice.

'Get up, heat the water. I will go and fetch milk,' he said as he went out of the door.

The next afternoon when Gauri's mother asked about the fight at night, the bride just evaded the subject. What could she say? She just said that Razzak had lost his mind yesterday and thrown her out of the house. Gauri's mother was shocked, 'What did you do then?'

'What could I do, Gauri's mother? I kept sitting on the threshold, shivering till I fell asleep.'

'What a life! I can't even say why you didn't come over to my place. Your husband would have just killed you if you had done that.'

'Let it be, it is over…let's talk about something pleasant.'

'Tell me, what should we talk about?'

'Ask your God to bless me with a son this time.'

'It will happen…definitely,' said Gauri's mother.

'Can I say something to you, Gauri's mother . . .?' the bride asked hesitantly.

'Tell me.'

'I wish that I have a son and I am able to educate my children just like you.'

'You must do it...if you want, I will help them get admission in school,' Gauri's mother reassured her.

'Will they admit my children?'

'Yes, why not? Gauri and her brother will also help them with their studies.'

The bride's heart was overwhelmed with the budding dream of being able to educate her children. This time she had a son, Mukim, and then another one, Salim. When she spoke to Razzak about sending the girls to school, he lost his temper completely, thrashed her and threw her out of the house. Gauri's mother began educating the bride's two daughters in her own house. When the bride was expecting her fifth child Mubina and Nargis would go to Gauri's house with their writing boards. They would toil the entire day over Maths and alphabet and at night their writing boards would be hidden away in the alcove.

When Mukim was five years old the bride spoke to Razzak about sending him to school. This time Razzak not only threw her and the children out of the house, but out of the alley. She was left at the roadside with her five children. After a while she sat down in the shade of a few office buildings wearing the white burqa which Nargis had picked up on her way out. This was the backside of the building where the windows were fitted with fans to gush out the warm air. She sat there on a parapet hiding her face from passersby till Razzak cooled down and she returned home.

During these three hours she had decided that, regardless of what happened, she was going to send Mukim to school. The next day she picked up her burqa and, accompanied by Nargis and Mukim, went and admitted the boy to the nearby school.

Gauri's mother was surprised. She asked, 'Did Razzak agree?'

'That ruffian is always throwing his weight around. What can we do? We can't stop living. He can beat us if he wants, but why should we tell him anyway? How involved is he with the house? He leaves in the morning and only shows his face late at night. We will just keep quiet.'

Gauri's mother was silent. She seemed a little distracted that day and said, 'We may not be able to talk in the afternoon for a few days.'

'Why, are you going somewhere?'

'No, my sister-in law's father-in-law is unwell. They are bringing him to Delhi to refer him to some hospitals. So, four people will be staying with us for a few days.'

'So that is why bhaisahib was helping you yesterday evening. I saw when I peeped in. You were handing him the clothes you had washed and he was putting them out to dry. He cares so much about you!'

'Everyone is helpful when they want something. Right now he will even stand on one leg for the entire day if he is asked to do so. It concerns his sister after all!'

'*Arre*, what are you saying...he often...'

'Only because he wants something, Dulhan...that's all! When my brother-in-law had an accident he had to undergo brain surgery. At that time my husband very clearly said that I should tell my sister to arrange for some accommodation on rent close to the hospital. "This place is too far and we don't have enough space," he had said. Now I would like to ask him that if she alone couldn't be accommodated in this house, then how are his sister's four family members going to fit in?' Gauri's mother expressed her annoyance.

'Where is bhaisahib right now?'

'He has gone to the station to receive them.'

'Forget about the past,' Dulhan said.

'I feel that the suffering of women will never lessen, it is just like the price of gold – always increasing.' Gauri's mother stared at Dulhan because she found her statement a bit puzzling. Actually Dulhan was merely trying to calm her down.

'Just think if our pain had been the price of potatoes and onions instead of gold it would at least have gone down sometime!' Both the women burst into laughter.

Their life went on, sharing each other's happiness and sorrow. The bride talked to Gauri's mother during the day and heard Mr Green's haunting melodies in the darkness of the night. Gauri's mother said that he was mourning the death of his Jesus Christ. Just like our *Muhurram*, thought the bride. Why do we like to participate in the sorrows of others? Sometimes we even get relief from pain by singing about it. Why? Do we quieten our own pain by singing about the pain of others? She did not know what the truth was but she had begun to understand that these melodies of the night were like a soothing balm to her burning soul.

The fact that Mukim was going to school could not be hidden from Razzak for very long. There was chaos at home. The bride found herself on the street again along with her children but Mukim continued to attend school. After a few years Salim also started accompanying him. The bride's alley would be bereft of the bride's presence; sometimes during searingly hot afternoons and sometimes during the cold nights, but the wheel of life kept moving on. As it always does!

One day, the children were delighted when another wheel was erected on the ground of the night shelter outside the mosque. Thinking that their mother might or might not agree to their request they pleaded with their elder sister Nargis to take them for a ride on the swings that had been set up. Nargis agreed to take on the responsibility but where was the money going to come from? She didn't have the guts to ask her mother. These days life was very difficult, anyway. Razzak was jobless. The day he managed to get some work, he would bring home some vegetables or mutton. Then they would buy a kilo of wheat and hundred grams of clarified butter and the kitchen stove would come to life. Otherwise, by the grace of God, there was always some roasted gram in the house.

Once the bride had quietly saved three pieces from last day's meat. She mixed them with the pieces of dry leftover rotis which had been kept aside, added some oil and spices and put them on fire to cook. Nargis asked, 'Will we have leftovers today?' She was told, 'You will be going to another house after you get married, learn to be careful with your words…tell the children we are cooking *haleem* and it just takes a little long to cook.' In such a situation how could Nargis gather the courage to ask for money for the swings!

Nargis had persuaded Mubina that since the two of them were the eldest they would forego the ride. Their youngest sister Nanhi was very small and there was the danger that she might get scared and start crying. So, it was finally decided that only Mukim and Salim would get a ride on the swings. Nargis hardened her heart. She had hidden the money left from the amount her younger aunt had gifted her under a trunk in the alcove. She took it out, tied it in a corner of her dupatta and, taking permission from her mother, set off for the night shelter in the middle of the afternoon. The bride raised her hands in prayer wishing that God would give everyone an elder sister like Nargis.

It was a June afternoon. Eddies of the hot summer wind were swirling around the corners of the doorless room. The bride unfurled the tarpaulin hanging outside the room using it as a curtain. It might make a difference. Then she came and lay down on the bed. The heat is unbearable and Nargis has taken the kids for a ride at this time as, she thought, the man who owned the swings is likely to charge less for the ride at a time when he may be sitting idle. She is so sensible despite being so young. She looks nice. Physical appearance is a gift of God but she has grown up to be a good-looking girl. Her chest is still not grown properly, thought the bride, but that is no cause for worry. Everything will be all right once she experiences the touch of a man after marriage.

Just then Razzak pushed aside the tarpaulin and entered the room. The bride sat up quickly. Razzak handed her a packet with almost a kilo of meat. The bride took it and moved aside the newspaper covering it before putting it in a dish. 'It is goat meat!' Her face reflected her astonishment. 'It seems you got some good work today.'

Razzak took off his kurta and hung it on a nail, 'No, I didn't get any work today, either.'

'Then how…this meat?'

'I went to Akbar's shop. He insisted that I take it.'

'What was the need to take it without payment?'

'We don't have to pay for it.'

'Then?'

'Just like that.'

The bride stood there, gaping in surprise. She picked up the packet of meat from the dish and tried to weigh it in her right hand. 'No one gives away 750 grams of meat just like that.'

'You think too much. Go and get me some water.' Razzak scolded her as he sat on the cot. When the bride returned with water he drank the entire glass in one go. 'Why are you rationing it like soup? Get some more.'

After drinking three glasses of water, it suddenly struck Razzak that his wife was all alone at home. 'Where are the children?' he asked.

'They will just be back,' she was evasive.

'Were you born the wrong way round? Can't you give a straight answer? I am asking you where are the children?' Razzak thundered.

'There is a swing opposite the mosque. They have gone there.'

'Opposite the mosque? Where? In the night shelter?'

'Yes.'

'Where are Nargis and Mubina?'

'They are the ones who have taken them. They must be on their way back.'

'Nargis has gone to the night shelter. Have you lost your senses? *Arre*, you are sitting here idle like a bull and you have sent a young girl out like this?'

'The children were insisting, so she took them…it isn't very far.'

'How dare you answer me back, you slut!' Razzak hit the bride on her cheek with his slippers so hard that she became dizzy. 'I am trying to marry her to Akbar and she is roaming around in the bazaar enjoying the swings.'

The bride regained her senses when she heard Razzak talking about Nargis' marriage. 'Akbar! That old widower already has two daughters.'

'Here she looks after four kids of yours, why won't she be able to take care of two there?'

'No!' The bride screamed with her hand covering her cheek. 'I won't let this happen.'

'You? You will stop me?'

'Are you a father or a butcher?'

'Come to your senses, you mad woman!' Razzak lowered his voice as he tried to convince her. 'Akbar's daughters will soon get married and leave the house. He has his own shop. The house, the shop, everything will belong to Nargis... and he has also offered me a job in his shop.'

'You want to sell your daughter?' The bride seemed to be possessed by the devil. She got up, picked the meat and threw it outside the tarpaulin towards the door. 'This is illicit in this house.'

Razzak pulled her towards him with her plait and started showering her with blows.The bride gathered her courage and shoved him away. 'It would have been better if you had taken your innocent child to the abbatoir and slaughtered her.'

'I will slaughter you first.' Razzak steadied himself, leapt towards the bride, pushed her against the wall and tried to throttle her. She managed to lift her knee and hit him in the groin forcing him to let go of her. For the first time in the fifteen or sixteen years of marriage, the bride had deliberately aimed a blow at Razzak. He bellowed in pain. When he headed towards her again, the bride warned him in a strict tone, 'Don't try to do this... this marriage will never take place.'

Razzak was filled with bloodlust. He caught hold of the bride's left arm and dragged her outside the door, 'Get out, you daughter of a whore! Go sit on the road.' He dragged her out of the alley spewing curses and then went back home.

The bride stood there for a while trying to calm her breathing. Each breath was reinforcing her determination. 'This wedding will never take place... never!' As she steadied her breathing she arranged her dishevelled hair and settled her dupatta on her head. She looked around. Like a typical June afternoon, everything wore a deserted look. In the tea shop Jamaal was sleeping with his head pillowed in his arms. The motor mechanic Siraj's shop was yawning with emptiness. She slowly moved towards the road. She crossed the street and sat down on the parapet behind the buildings. Gusts of hot summer wind were buffeting her from all sides but she was sitting there, unmindful, thinking deeply as the saliva dried in her mouth. Just thinking.

Who knew what thoughts were running through the mind of the bride who had once again been thrown out of her house that day! What hadn't she done and borne for Razzak! She had squeezed herself dry. And Razzak scraped her off like the skin off a goat's back and threw her out of her home. The blasts of hot air suddenly seemed to age the bride. Now he is determined to ruin her daughter's life as well, she thought. Abbu used to say that till a goat is alive, it keeps bleating me, me, me... but once it is dead and its skin is used to card wool, it makes the sound you, you, you... Living all his life with goats even Razzak has learnt to say me, me, me all the time. He is so selfish that he never thinks of anyone else.

Something within her was boiling. Oh! He will even marry off his daughter for his own selfish reasons. She adjusted her dupatta, which was being blown about in the hot wind, to hide the mark of the slipper on her cheek. Her life had become like Mukim's game of snakes and ladders where nights and days were playing one unknown move after another. Sometimes the day was bitten by a snake and at other times the night was swallowed by one as it tried to climb a ladder. Or someone tumbled down a stair. That day she had fallen down the afternoon stair and been thrown out on the road. Who wants this disgusting offal-like life where one could be thrown out at any time? The bride twisted her neck as though she was rejecting life itself though she knew that she would have to go back to her old existence. Right back inside its entrails.

Just then she spotted Nargis coming along with the sleeping Nanhi in her arms. As soon as Nargis spotted her mother she quickened her steps.

'Ammi, you are here? Has Abbu returned?' she said spontaneously. The bride kept quiet.

'Nanhi had slept. I thought I would drop her home.'

The bride didn't say anything. She just kept staring at Nargis' innocent face. There was a storm raging inside her. Nargis couldn't understand what was happening, so she kept standing there gently rocking her sister.

Despite being out on the road they had gone back to the world of their own alley when they heard a voice, 'Where is the bride' s alley, sister?' Moving her gaze away from Nargis, the bride looked towards the road and saw an elderly, tired-looking man with a bicycle. Nargis also looked at him and then at her mother.

'*Arre,* listen, this bride's alley…' The old man had only begun to repeat his question when the bride, who was sitting outside the alley, gestured and said, 'There…on the other side of the road.' Then she got up, took Nanhi from Nargis and sat down on the parapet once again. Nargis found this very strange. She sat down next to her mother and wiped the beads of sweat from her forehead. The bride's breath had calmed down but, within her, their echoes were beating a staccato rhythm, repeating the same thought, in the same voice, 'Never…never…never.'

The bride and her daughter looked at the middle-aged man with the cycle making his way into the bride's alley. An alley without a board, a bride's alley in name only!

Dhampur

Wonder why days and nights are an unalienable part of life, just like legends? They follow each other, one after another, never seeming to end. Expending their lives, pursuing each other. Does the night chase the day, or is it the day that wanders around looking for the nights which succeed sorrowful evenings retreating from daylight? The darkness increases, swallowing the doors and windows of the whole house, without even stopping to chew them. It is a hungry beggar, Nitya thought to herself as she turned over on the bed. The roots of the mind are also very dark, entangled with one another. How can one see through such darkness? They say there are seven subterranean worlds. How many such worlds lie below the realm of the mind!

How could Nitya deal with the turmoil inside her? All she could do was, turn restlessly from one side to the other like someone stirring a pot of boiling milk to prevent it from spilling over. It seemed the fire and the tumult would only ebb with the dawn. Everyone awaits the gleam of daybreak even if it is stricken with frost. She would also see a dawn the next day. Time which is just a few hours away is also called 'tomorrow', but then what else can it be called? Just as her house was called a 'home' because it was one. So, the next day she had to go back home. Her own home.

She remembered the time when the word 'home' was like a beautiful recurrent dream in her mind. 'Home is an aspiration, a desire, and having one of your own is a profound experience.' This was what she had written with a lipstick on one of the large mirrored-doors of the almirah that day when she had first decorated Chandramohan's room in Ghaziabad and transformed it into a home. Now why did the same word 'home' bubble in her mind like boiling rice. Suddenly, she sat up and told herself not to think about all this. The next day she had to return home, her own home.

Suddenly, she shrugged the thought of home off her mind and picked up her pillow and came out into the open. Perhaps her mind would be able to breathe more freely here. She spread out the rush mat standing against a wall of the courtyard, placed her pillow on it and tried to lie down. The moon, shining with the mild luminosity of the thirteenth day of the dark half of the lunar month, seemed to be looking at her. In that dim light she felt as though she had become an image of stone or an ancient ruin which lived both in the past and in the present.

An old yellowed memory floated into her mind. Prabha bua sitting on a string cot on the roof of that very house embroidering a pillowslip and young Nitya sitting with an open book in her lap admiring the word 'welcome' and roses embroidered on the pillow cover. Prabha bua was working on the green thorns around the rose.

'Bua, how does one do such beautiful embroidery?'

'How would I know...ask the needle.'

Wrinkling up her nose in disgust Nitya buried her face in the book. Prabha bua was smiling. Pulling the thread upwards with the needle, she asked, 'Are you reading a story? Is it good?'

'How would I know? Ask the book!' Nitya answered laughing so uproariously at her own wit that Prabha bua stopped her work to stare at her. And then her laughter was no longer solitary.

Nitya's childhood was closely linked to Prabha bua. What was Prabha bua's relationship with her, apart from being an aunt, her father's sister? She was an elder sister, a younger mother, an older friend, maybe everything or nothing at all, because like the others even Nitya did not know where Prabha bua...Nitya's thoughts abruptly shivered to a halt. She remembered the letter sent by Prabha bua many years ago from Dhampur in which she had written only one quotation in her beautiful small handwriting – 'Within all of us lies immeasurable space which has not been mapped or explored. If we want to understand the turbulence and turmoil which exist inside us, we must pay attention to this immense space as well.' At the end she had written – 'I am not writing the name of the author because you don't have to appear for an exam, nor does it make any difference.' She had not even signed her own name at the bottom of the letter. Perhaps that was of no significance, either!

The world of the mind is full of the clamour of images, events and words. These frequently bump into each other even as they attempt to avoid contact. Sometimes, a word searches for an image which sits leaning its head upon the shoulders of an event, or an image pursues a happening which hides, motionless, in the shadow of a group of words.

That day, in the dim light of the moon, resting her head upon the pillow slip embroidered by her aunt, Nitya wanted to recall all those moments when she really discovered Prabha bua. But where could she find those lost moments? The moments of the present smiled feebly as though apologising for all those innumerable moments which had already been massacred. Prabha bua often used to say, 'Nitu, history is not meant to be forgotten but to be repeatedly brought into mind.' Nitu tried to follow the memories of the past just as one tries to chase the sun in winter. But then how much of the winter sun does one manage to capture!

The family of Prabha bua's father Kalicharan had moved from Hapur to Delhi after Kalicharan's elder sister Prano Devi was married to Ambika Dutt. Both these orphaned young children had been brought up by their uncle. Though Kalicharan was two years younger to his sister he was married off earlier because his aunt wanted him to marry her brother's daughter. However, it took a while to find a boy for Prano. Finally, a proposal came from Ambika Dutt of Delhi – a man who had already lost two wives. Their good luck lay in the fact that the gentleman had already received two lavish dowries but had no children. The third time he did not have much interest in dowry, so Prano Devi, despite being an orphan, became a part of his well-to-do household.

Prano Devi was deeply attached to her younger brother, Kalicharan or Kali. Soon, she managed to persuade Ambika Dutt to invite Kali and his family to live with her. At that moment Kalicharan only had his wife, and a son Dwarka Prasad in his family. Ambika Dutt owned a flour mill. The work was increasing every day and he urgently needed someone to take over the job of a manager if he wanted to save his life from being disfigured by the dust and chaff of the wheat. In such a situation, it was impossible for him to get a more trustworthy and reliable manager than his brother-in-law. And then, the relationship being what it was, Kali would be obliged to accept any salary without quibbling. He would never have the nerve to ask for more and Prano Devi would also remain perpetually indebted to her husband.

The rest of Kalicharan's three children, Saroj Bala, Prehlad Prasad and Prabha Bala were born in the environs of the flour mill in Delhi. Prano Devi ruled vigorously over the household and Ambika Dutt governed their lives with equal authority. Which child attended which school or college, how much he or she studied – all these decisions were ultimately taken by Ambika Dutt. He had only one son who did not burden him with the necessity of taking any such decisions on his behalf. The son left school after the eighth class and assumed the responsibility of becoming the local bully. His behaviour prompted Prano Devi to speak to her husband and Ambika Dutt immediately decided to involve him in the working of the mill. Keeping his nature and disposition in mind, he was assigned the task of collecting dues – a job which he cheerfully accepted. Gradually he began to control all the finances of the enterprise and fill his own pockets. His poor uncle Kalicharan was left helplessly scrutinising the incomplete pages of the company account books. He continued to draw the salary decided upon many years ago which, like an old and tattered covering, barely fulfilled the needs of his growing family. One month Dwarka Prasad would grow out of his salary and another month it would be Prehlad Prasad. However, life progressed with relative peace of mind under the shelter of Prano Devi's love and affection.

The first voice of revolt was raised by Prehlad Prasad when he refused to work in the flour mill. He had decided to do B.Sc.

in Physics. The thought of doing B.A. in accounts like Dwarka Prasad, and dreaming of the mill day after day was unbearable to him. He managed to get his way as far as the B.Sc. was concerned but when he pushed to do his Master's, Ambika Dutt decided to put his foot down. He decided to cut off all financial assistance which the boy received from the family. Prehlad now began to support his studies by doing tuitions. There was no rancour in his heart. On the contrary, he was quite happy. He had never imagined that he would be able to escape from the mill so easily. His home lay within the environs of the mill but his world was outside it.

The only member of the family who had access to this world was Prabha Bala who was Nitya's Prabha bua. Prabha was only three years younger to her brother Prehlad. She was good at studies but in keeping with the wishes of Ambika Dutt she had been enrolled in a tailoring course after passing the eleventh class. She enjoyed embroidery and stitching but her real interest lay in the books she borrowed from her Prehlad bhaisahib. The fiction and romances which Prehlad bhaisahib brought home were never returned until Prabha had read all of them. She had even visited Delhi University with her brother a few times and the library which was as big as the flour mill. She also enjoyed going to the Delhi Public Library near the railway station with Prehlad bhaisahib.

Sometimes bhaisahib would go into another direction leaving her alone near the book shelves. Alone in that vast room, surrounded by innumerable books she would feel a strange arid fear. So many books, so many stories, so much knowledge! Many ideas must be refuting and challenging each other. But they are all sitting here quietly, without even a shadow of dissention. Isn't it strange that opposing ideas can sit side by side, mutely, in the same room without any debate or argument? When words become silent they alter their character, and the opposite is also true, for when silent words speak up they too change their character. Prabha Bala gently caressed one word after another, just to determine whether the words would speak up when they were touched. Prabha bua told Nitya all this one day standing in a silent corner of the Delhi Public library. At that time Prabha was not married.

Nitya also knew that Prehlad chacha would sometimes take Prabha bua to Regal or Odeon or for a film festival to see a movie, pretending that they were going to the library. Later Prabha bua would narrate the entire story of the film to Nitya when they were all alone on the roof.

Prehlad chacha became a lecturer in a college within a few years. Prabha bua used to carry this victory of his around like a brooch on a sari. He had been working for around six months when the fateful day arrived. He went to Assam on a college trip. One day one of the boys suddenly slipped and fell into the Lohit river. Prehlad Prasad also jumped in trying to save him. And then neither of them was ever found. A glimmering window in Prabha's life was suddenly slammed shut, leaving her bereft. Nitya's grandmother could not bear the shock of her son's death and she too, passed away.

Dwarka Prasad, Prabha's elder brother, had two children by then – Mukesh and Nitya. Saroj Bala, the elder sister, was married and had gone to Bareilly. She also had a daughter. Prabha bala, who was a couple of years younger to Prehlad, was many years younger to Dwarka Prasad and Saroj Bala. However, she was nearly twenty years old and Prano Devi was very concerned about the marriage of this motherless niece of hers. She spoke to Kali and made him pay more attention to this matter. Somehow, it proved to be quite difficult to get a suitable groom for Prabha, and if one was found there was a very high demand for dowry. Ambika Dutt was also becoming a little lax and was gradually losing control over the mill. His son was regularly showing a loss in the financial registers.

The doors of the house would open hopefully to welcome prospective bridegrooms and their families, and then quickly close behind them as they departed. Sometimes, one opens a door expecting to see someone but finds someone unexpected standing there instead. Similarly, one day Saroj's husband and Prabha bua's brother-in-law Dushyant jijaji arrived from Bareilly. He had been sent to Delhi for six months of training by his company. For Kalicharan, the absence of a young man in the house due to Prehlad's death was now filled by Dushyant Kumar. He was tall, well-built and had the knack of narrating every incident like an interesting story. The sea of silence that had invaded Prabha bua's life was thrown into turmoil. She had the responsibility of looking after Dushyant, keeping his likes and dislikes in mind. When her jijaji left home looking dashing and handsome, her eyes would follow him. At that moment she felt as though she was looking at Prehlad, not at Dushyant. This was something jijaji could never understand, neither could Janaki bhabhi, who felt it her duty to warn Saroj, her elder sister-in-law. She wrote to her asking her to come to Delhi. When she arrived Janaki bhabhi pointed at Prabha and remarked to Saroj, 'Bibi, look after your house. Men are so fickle. God knows what kind of training will take place here while you are in Bareilly.' Saroj Bala became wary. Kalicharan was now quite old and was suffering from diabetes. Saroj sought the help of Dwarka Prasad and the search for a groom for Prabha acquired a new urgency.

It was decided that it would be better for Prabha to be away from the city, so they looked for a boy outside Delhi. Soon, Prabha bua was engaged to be married to Radheyshyam who was head clerk in the income-tax office in the small town of Dhampur. Both sides were equally anxious to have an early wedding. When Prabha bua was dressed as a bride, she examined herself in the mirror. Nitya noticed the slight smile on her lips. She pulled at the edge of Prabha bua's sari and told her affectionately, 'Bua, you are looking pretty.'

Prabha bua answered almost brazenly, 'That is true.'

Nitya found her frankness a little odd. She wanted to know what was going on in her bua's mind. 'Bua, what are you thinking about?'

'Nothing, I was remembering my mother. She used to say that the worst thing that can happen to a girl from Delhi, or a cow from Mathura, is to be sent away from her hometown.' Prabha bua let out a short laugh, 'Do you know she was from a village near Delhi and went to Hapur after her marriage?' After a while she added gravely, 'But her luck changed and the entire family came back to Delhi.'

Nitya was shaken to the core. She could not meet Prabha's eyes but she held on to her hand and said, 'Papa says Dhampur is a nice place…look, the colour of your henna is so beautiful.'

'Just like Dhampur,' Prabha bua said, pulling her hand away as she walked ahead.

Even before Prabha arrived in Dhampur to become a member of the head-clerk's extended family her ill-luck had begun. The house already had two elder brothers-in-law, their wives and children. There were also two sisters-in-law – one unmarried and the other a young widow. The sisters-in-law were either dedicated to the kitchen or jewellery. Prabha's simple handloom saris, many bought at the Khadi Bhandar sale, and her lack of ostentatious jewellery set her apart from the other women of the household, like a black cardamom in a yellow curry. Radheyshyam, the head-clerk, was a typical small-town Romeo. He was fond of having a good time and saw every new movie within a week of its release with his friends. When his sisters-in law teased him saying 'What sort of an ascetic have you brought home?', he would feel even more alienated from Prabha.

Prabha who used to accompany Prehlad bhaisahib to plays in Sapru House, or English movies like *Ben-Hur* which she did not fully understand, could not find any enjoyment in occasional trips to the typically small-town Dhampur bazaar. There was only one hope left – that the birth of a child would help her to reconcile to life in Dhampur. But this hope did not materialise for quite some time. Finally, one day Radheyshyam babu took Prabha to Delhi for a series of medical tests and examinations. As soon as the doctors arrived at the conclusion that it was not Prabha but Radheyshyam who was responsible for the couple's childlessness, Radheyshyam abandoned the tests and returned to Dhampur rarely showing his face in Delhi, or in the house of his in-laws thereafter.

In fact, Radheyshyam's aversion to his in-laws even extended to Prabha. He seemed to revert to the days of his youth; his moustache acquired greater dimensions and he attempted to assert his masculinity by spending most of his evenings away from home.

His relationship with Prabha was near the end of its tether but the household generally put the blame on the wife. During this time one day when Prabha opened her little box she discovered that all her jewellery was missing. When the news of the theft reached Delhi, everyone was stunned.

'What theft? There is barely any room in that house. Three small rooms, and more people than possessions! There is hardly any place to put down your foot...when did the thief enter the house? He must have given it to some woman of his...' said Kalicharan, wiping his mouth with the ends of his muffler as he lay on the bed he occupied in his old age.

Dushyant Kumar had been transferred to Delhi and had settled there with his family. Prabha Bala had been married for only five years when she got the news that jijaji had died in an accident. The shock of this tragedy, coming after the death of Prehlad bhaisahib, devastated Prabha. After her marriage she had only met her sister Saroj occasionally on festivals and that too, generally amidst a crowd of relatives. During the mourning for jijaji, when Prabha moved towards Saroj to console her, she pushed her aside with her elbow. Despite Dushyant Kumar's death, Saroj had evidently not been able to erase the old incident from her mind, or perhaps Dushyant had been in the habit of occasionally referring to Prabha in glowing terms and this had wounded Saroj. Dushyant's death had provided Prabha with the possibility of mourning for her brother once again but this time she had to return home discomfited, nursing the pain in her heart. These two tragic incidents made her feel even more detached from life.

Saroj Bala's daughter went abroad after her marriage. Saroj had Dushyant Kumar's pension and his house but her loneliness was not assuaged by these. Janaki bhabhi was not likely to let such an opportunity slip by, therefore it was decided that Saroj Bala would live with her and Dwarka Prasad and would give them the rent she earned from her house to pay for her upkeep. Her husband's pension was enough to pay for Saroj's needs. In this manner, not only did Janaki bhabhi's financial situation improve considerably but she could also try to convince everyone about how supportive and concerned she and her husband were about their widowed sister.

Nitya had finished her schooling and wanted to study a foreign language. However, as she did not get admission in a regular college she started doing her B.A. by correspondence. Besides every evening she attended the three-year German language course in Max Mueller Bhavan. She also started learning music from the Sangeet Kala Kendra.

Chandramohan was a talented young man from the interior of Bihar who came with his theatre group to Delhi for a visit but then settled down permanently in the city. Other boys from his village, who were studying in Delhi, had taken a room on rent in Katwaria Sarai. Chandramohan also joined them. He had a good grasp on music, so he soon started getting work to provide music for plays and cultural programmes.

Nitya and Chandramohan decided to get married after they had been friends for nearly two years. Nitya wanted to test Prabha bua's reaction to her decision before sharing it with the rest of the family. Ambika Dutt had passed away nearly a year ago but she was stunned at the response she got from Prabha, 'Look, Neetu, think carefully before you say anything at home. Uncle has not yet departed from this house, nor is he going anywhere... this house belonged to him and it will always remain his... I am afraid...'

'What?'

'I'm afraid they may marry you off to someone in Dhampur as well in their anger.' Then after a while she added softly, 'God knows how long babujis and other elders like him will rule over households.'

Nitya's decision stunned her father Dwarka Prasad. Before Janaki could react, Saroj Bala started turning the beads of her rosary agitatedly, 'Neither caste nor community…and works as an actor! Couldn't she find anyone else in the world?'

Nitya finished her German course around this time and started getting work as a translator. She would leave home in the morning, spend the day in a library, and return home in the evening. She required no financial support from her family. In these circumstances, at the urging of Mukesh, Nitya was married to Chandramohan despite a complete lack of enthusiasm in the family.

The two of them spent the first fifteen or twenty days after their marriage in the room at Katwaria Sarai which had been vacated by Chandramohan's friends, who had temporarily shifted to their friends' rooms in JNU. This arrangement could not last too long and soon Chandramohan rented a room at a nominal amount in the house of his friend in Ghaziabad. Nitya now shifted from Delhi to her home in Ghaziabad.

Soon the leaves began to turn brown. In Delhi spring is surpassed by autumn very quickly. During the long melancholic afternoons one could hear only the sound of one's own footsteps on the leaves scattered on the wide, silent streets of Mandi house.

Chandramohan was quite busy with his theatre group. Nitya had started working in a private company, so she had to travel to Delhi. Whenever she was free she would do her translations. Both of them were busy trying to improve the financial situation of the household. Days, months and years passed like empty carriages before their eyes. Nitya now had the memories of Chandramohan's companionship rather than Chandramohan himself for company.

Living with memories is just an illusion. Whenever Nitya spoke to him about starting a family Chandramohan avoided the topic. If Nitya referred to the matter more seriously he would blow on the tendrils of her hair and remark, 'I am not in the mood to become a father yet, my dear.' If Nitya maintained a stony silence, he would try to persuade her, 'Let us first get settled properly. We haven't been married for very long...don't think about all this...concentrate on your job...pay attention to the foreign delegations...do more translations...you know, darling, money....money is the real necessity of life.'

'Once the child is here, the money will also come.'

'Don't talk rubbish! Think big...we can always have children. Concentrate on your work.'

At such moments she would remember Prabha bua. Once when she had come from Dhampur she had told Nitya very sadly, 'Nitu, you didn't see your grandmother...do you know she didn't have a nail on her forefinger? I used to find that finger of hers very strange. I would often ask her, "Amma, why doesn't this finger have a nail, is it broken?" She would reply, "No, it hasn't been there since I was born." '

'Since birth?' Nitya had remarked in amazement.

'Yes, then once I asked her why is the nail missing? And she answered, "Because I am a mother. Anyone who is a good mother doesn't have a nail on this finger." '

'Why?' Nitya asked with childish curiosity.

'I asked her the same question. "Why?" She replied, "So that I can apply kajal to my children's eyes without worrying.

If anything gets stuck in their throats, I can quickly pull it out without hurting them." ' Nitya listened eagerly.

'And you know, Nitu, I thought what she said was true. I would check the forefinger of every woman who visited us very carefully. But everyone's nails were intact and I felt very happy at the thought that my mother was the best mother. There was no one else like her.' Prabha bua had suddenly become silent. She had looked at the nail on her forefinger, 'Look, Nitu, my forefinger has a nail but I could never even become a mother, not better or worse…just nothing.'

Nitya felt that sediment of sorrow which seeped from Prabha bua's body to her mind had now passed on to her. She checked her own forefinger and then turned her eyes away. Who knew what fate had in store?

Chandramohan often went out of Delhi with the theatre groups and whenever there was less translation work Nitya would go to her parents' house. Saroj Bala's influence over Janaki had grown to such an extent that even Nitya was silenced by the changed environment at home. There was no one with whom she could share her marital problems, and in any case her marriage had been her own decision. One day she overheard Saroj bua whispering, 'Bhabhi, be careful, it doesn't seem right for Nitya to come and stay so often.'

'I am sure everything is fine…otherwise she would have said something,' Janaki had whispered back.

'What can she say, and how can she complain? But these are not good signs. One can understand it if she is expecting or is ill but I cannot understand why a married girl should visit her parents so frequently.'

Saroj Bala used to give Dwarka Prasad some money from her pension if the need arose. This was a big support for the family.

After the death of Ambika Dutt his son had taken over the flour mill. Dwarka Prasad had been reduced to a mere employee. Kalicharan had also finally left his bed and passed away. Mukesh only managed to hold onto a job for a few months, he had not yet been able to settle in life or in employment.

Even before Nitya's marriage Saroj Bala's growing assertiveness had increased Prabha's solitude and sadness. After her marriage, despite the fact that her brother and sister-in-law were not very welcoming, Prabha would often come on festivals and birthdays and try to build the bridges of relationships. When she entered the house saying 'Happy Dussehra, bhabhi' Janaki would lower her head under the pretext of pulling her sari over it and mutter under her breath, 'Here she is again, now she will be stuck here for at least three or four days.' Then she would stand up and embrace Prabha saying, 'Welcome, Bibi, you have come after so many days. Nitya is really fond of you...she remembers you very often.'

After a day or two Prabha bua would tell Nitya, 'When I leave, just take out a handloom sari for me...even an old one will do.' Nitya would always feel very depressed while handing over the sari. Anyway, those were all old memories. Nitya had already been married for five years now. Two years ago she had bought a blue, black and white sari for Prabha with the intention of giving it to her at their next meeting, even before bua could ask for one.. 'Bua, your sari! I have bought it with my own salary.' They say that thoughts follow one around like ghosts. But in Nitya's case it was the handloom sari which haunted her; she never saw Prabha bua again, nor for that matter did anyone else.

The last time when Nitya met Prabha she was astonished by what she saw. One hot summer afternoon, Prabha had entered the house with a cloth bag slung over her shoulder. Nitya was meeting her for the first time after her own wedding. Prabha's skin had become rough and tanned. When everyone dispersed for a nap after lunch, Nitya persuaded Prabha to go with her to the bathroom and gave her a bath, scrubbing her to peel off the layers of dirt. There was so much dirt that Nitya had to keep on pouring water over Prabha. The drain was flooded with soap scum and layers of dirt. Prabha bua burst out laughing loudly, 'Look at the flood of dirt...it looks as though Dhampur will get washed away like the water in the drain.'

Then she wore an old sari of Nitya and both of them sat under the draft of the cooler. Gradually she stretched out her legs and relaxed against the pillow. She closed her eyes and as her mind wandered off to some unknown destination, she slowly called out to Nitya who was lying next to her, 'Nitu.'

'Yes, Bua.'

'Nitu, you know everyone has a heart and there is a nameplate on it. The nameplate on my heart...sometimes I want to turn it upside down, reverse it because it has sorrow written on it...but then I don't do it.' Nitya's sleep had fled away. She was lying on her side with her eyes closed, feeling the presence of Prabha bua. Her ears heard, 'Do you know why? Because behind the nameplate is written – happiness. If I turn the nameplate over, happiness will come to the front and sorrow will shift to the back, clinging to the walls of my heart, closer than it was before.'

Prabha bua was not feeling sleepy. Perhaps she had become accustomed to the sleeping pills which Radheyshyam uncle used to give her frequently. It must have been convenient for him to keep Prabha in a state of somnolence. Her body would remain alive while the passions of her heart would be stilled. Nitya thought to herself with a sarcastic smile on her lips. How would he understand that the passions of the mind cannot be quietened? They can just change direction sometimes...moving towards a dead end, aimless and unfocused.

In any case directionless paths were becoming a part of Prabha bua's life. 'I like wandering on the roads, Nitu...I like it very much and I especially like crying on the roads...houses belong to people...some have one, some don't. Some have less, others have more...but the road belongs to everyone . . .equally...so it also belongs to me.'

Will she come across a weeping Prabha bua sitting by the side of a road some day? Nitya remembered something else Prabha had said, 'Do you know, Nitu, sometimes at home when everyone else is having their meals, I eat only fruits because they are just like the roads...they belong to everyone and no one.'

Mukesh said that she often came away from Dhampur without informing anyone. At such times he used to escort her to the bus stop and put her on the bus to Dhampur. After a month or so she would be back again. She would leave her bag at home and wander in the streets. When she was tired she would sit down and watch people coming and going around her, and return home late at night. In the morning Mukesh would bundle her into a three-wheeler, take her to the bus stop and put her on the bus to Dhampur.

'Dhampur,' Nitya repeated the word with tears in her eyes and a thin smile on her trembling face. What is this Dhampur? *Dham* means a place to stay – a home, and *pur* means a settlement, also a place to live – a home. Both *dham* and *pur*? Home twice over? Nitya remembered how as a child one of the games she used to play was 'house'. Little girls often hear their friends repeating the sentence, 'Let's play *ghar-ghar*' and then once they reach the threshold of adulthood the same sentence is repeated by their parents and elders, 'come and play *ghar-ghar*.' House meaning 'home', meaning 'Dhampur'! Something which is not real but make-believe, like any imaginary game. An illusion which constantly gives the impression of truth, a reality for which and with the support of which women spend their entire lives. An illusion women have been running after for centuries!

There is another *dham* which is the body where the soul resides. It doesn't have any *pur* attached to it but it also slips away gradually, almost imperceptibly. Despite our knowledge that this home – our body – is transient, we take care of it, live for it, suffer for it. Though we beg God for deliverance from the illusion that is life, yet how difficult it is to leave it!

The last time Prabha bua came from Dhampur, she reached home at seven in the morning. She had either travelled by the night bus or had spent the night at some religious guest house or *dharamshala*. As soon as she entered Janaki bhabhi said irritably, 'Bibi, why can't you live in peace at your own home? There are disagreements in every house over one thing or the other…one doesn't run away every time one is upset.'

'No, Bhabhi, there hasn't been any disagreement. Who am I to be upset with anyone!' Prabha answered and then added in a soft voice, 'I am upset only with myself. I try to calm myself but…'

'What will phoophaji think?' Mukesh remarked.

'Beta, he has a lot of things to think about. Don't worry about him, I am not staying on.'

'Come, I will put you on the bus…go back to Dhampur,' Mukesh said.

'*Arre*, beta, how many times will you send me back to Dhampur? Now my body is tired…I don't feel like staying here.

Make arrangements for me in any place of pilgrimage, or if you know someone in Haridwar…' Prabha bua said, as she sank down exhausted on the floor and leaned against the wall clutching her bundle-like bag.

'Listen, you make some tea,' Dwarka Prasad instructed Janaki as he came out of his room, 'give Prabha some tea and refreshments…this time I will personally escort her to Dhampur.'

'All right, Bhaisahib, it is fine,' Prabha said. Then she gathered her strength and stood up, 'Bhabhi, make some tea, I will just be back.' She got ready to go out.

'*Arre,* where are you going?' Dwarka Prasad asked in a thunderous voice.

'Nowhere, Bhaisahib, I will go and get some biscuits of my choice from the market. Bhabhi, make some tea…I will just be back with the biscuits.' Prabha bua departed in the direction of the market with her bag slung over her shoulder. But she never came back. She did not reach Dhampur, nor did anyone ever see her. Who knew where Prabha bua was lost and what had happened to her! Maybe she was living like a vagrant in some *dharamshala,* or wandering on the streets aimlessly. How could one find out? Newspapers do not publish details of all the unclaimed bodies that were found. Nitya was waiting for her, even this day, with the blue, white and black handloom sari and an increasingly crippled hope.

Nitya was also waiting since the evening for the arrival of the morning. There was a faint orange glow in the sky. Often this light, this sunshine halts at the very threshold of the mind, she thought. Inside there are glimmers of light and shades of darkness, just like the dusk. Nitya searched within her mind in the light of memories of the past. How long will this shadow war continue? All her life?

Every morning, she opened her eyes to a new day which was not her own and she had to live through the 'alien-ness' of the day. When she needed a day of her own she couldn't find it anywhere near her. Perhaps she was only fated to have as much of the day as the tiny pinch of salt one adds to flour or sometimes even forgets to add.

And Prabha bua? Even her nights were scorned, yet they must have seemed her own dark nights just like her benighted life. Did she ever consider scrubbing them, washing them till they became bright, making them her days? What would she do with all those chaotic dreams stored in the alcoves of her nights? Nitya thought that Prabha bua would tuck them away in her blouse. There they would be safely hidden from the day. In any case it must be years since anyone peeped in there.

The morning had arrived. Nitya had her breakfast in a strange frame of mind. Everyone thought she was anxious to return home. They helped her in her work and she left for the bus stop with Mukesh, after saying goodbye to everyone. The bus for Ghaziabad was standing there and some passengers were already seated in it. The conductor was standing near the bus trying to gather some more passengers. 'Ghaziabad... Ghaziabad,' he shouted.

Nitya walked swiftly in that direction with Mukesh following her. The conductor saw her and got ready to give her a ticket, 'One or two? Where do you want to go?'

Mukesh had just put his hand in his pocket to pull out his wallet when Nitya gave the conductor the fifty rupee note she had clutched in her hand, 'One ticket... Dhampur.'

Mukesh stopped searching his pocket. 'Nitu?' He stared at her, forgetting that his hand was still in his pocket. The conductor repeated in a surprised tone, 'Dhampur?' But Nitya took the ticket from his hand and, slinging her bag over her shoulder, boarded the bus without a backward glance. The conductor shrugged his shoulders and got into the bus. The driver started the engine when he heard the whistle and the bus moved...towards Ghaziabad or Dhampur...who knows?

Buses generally travel to predetermined destinations and carry their passengers wherever they want to go. But Nitya? Though she had boarded the bus to go to her Dhampur she had no idea whether it would really take her to her destination. She might even get off midway. She would take the decision now that she was in the bus. For the time being, she had bid farewell to all those people who always and in every way ensured that the daughters of the house were put on the bus to Dhampur.

The Omnipresent Maulshree

'One day the sun and the moon were playing together. Suddenly, the sun spied a twinkling rosy star very far away. He forgot to play and started looking towards it.'

'Then?'

'Then a bad man came and quietly threw a black cloth over the moon, wrapped it into a bundle and stole it away.'

'Who was that bad man?' asked the eyes wide with fear.

'He was a demon,' came the answer.

'What was his name?'

'Name? His name was Asur…' The name suddenly popped in Radhika's mind .

'Then?' the wide eyes asked again.

'When the sun turned around to tell the moon about the rosy star he found the moon had disappeared.'

The tiny eyes widened some more with astonishment.

'He thought the moon was being naughty and had gone and hidden himself behind some clouds. The sun roamed around the sky calling out, "Moon, O Moon, dear Moon, where are you?" But he got no answer.'

'What did the sun do then?' Maulshree asked, looking attentively at Radhika's face.

'The sun realised that the moon must be in trouble. He was very unhappy at having lost his dear friend. He realised he would have to ask someone for help, so he thought of Shiva. He ran to look for him and told him that the moon had been stolen by someone.'

'Then?'

'First Shiva was a little worried but then he tried to think coolly about what should be done. He closed his eyes and concentrated. He saw that the moon had been imprisoned in a dark tiny room by a demon called Asur, who was planning to eat it up in the night.'

'Then?'

'Then Shiva got angry. He said to the sun, "Now I am not going to forgive Asur. He has done something terrible today." Both of them went to meet Asur. When Asur saw how angry Shiva was, he was a little frightened in the beginning but then he gathered his courage and shouted, "Go back both of you. I am not going to free the moon. I have been wanting to eat this cool and sweet moon for a long time. Go back."'

'Then what did Shiva do?' came the question.

'Shiva became mad with anger. He said, "Asur, you had better count your last breath now" and he turned the demon into stone.'

'You mean he cursed him?'

'Yes.'

'If you curse someone, you turn him into stone?' Maulshree asked innocently.

'No, one can do many other things but this is what Shiva did to Asur.'

'Then?'

'Then the sun quickly opened the door of the dark room. Inside he saw the moon had been wrapped up in a bundle. He took him out and embraced him. Then both of them came back to the sky. All the stars were waiting for them there. They were all very happy. They all played together and had a lot of fun.'

'What did they play?'

'Some game.'

'Which one?'

'Game? They…they played Ring a Ring o' Roses. And that is the end of the story.'

'Tell me some more,' Maulshree said enthusiastically.

'No! Now my pussy cat is going to close her eyes and go to sleep,' Radhika said, placing her fingers on Maulshree's eyes. Maulshree caught her wrist, pushed it aside and asked with a sparkle in her eyes, 'Mama, from where do you get all these stories in your throat?'

'Come on, pussy, go to sleep quickly now.' Radhika slapped her cheek playfully and lay down beside her.

✦

The morning had not yet swum through the night to Radhika's door when she awoke. She had probably left the tap open at night. The intermittent sound of water dripping into the bucket and the occasional gurgle of the tap told her that another morning had arrived. She had waited for this morning for a long time. Many such mornings had come and would come in the future. That morning she had to go to Maulshree's school to meet her teacher. The parent-teacher meeting was actually scheduled to be held the next day but she had been called that day. Maulshree had been promoted from the first to the second class but Radhika recalled that, as Maulshree's mother, she had always been called one day ahead or after the PTA meeting ever since her daughter was in nursery.

She had never worried about Maulshree's studies. It was not Radhika's dream that Maulshree should always come first in her class. She had not been admitted to this school to earn any medals. Yes, there was a hope that she would grow to be a good human being but perhaps this was a difficult desire because it was not so easy to achieve. Radhika had not yet understood that for a hope to flower one needs not merely fertile soil but also a good environment and the manure of values and ideas. And sometimes this manure, however good it is, becomes a weed. She glanced at the bed next to hers. She could see Maulshree's innocent, carefree face. Her eyes were closed and her hair was spread out. Suddenly Radhika's heart was filled with love and she pushed her hair away with gentle hands.

Sometimes she was drenched inside by her understanding of the depths of Maulshree's little mind. And then a shiver of fear would come back to her. Why wasn't her daughter like other children, or were other children just like her daughter? She knew that there was a land of jungles in Maulshree's mind. There were many different jungles in it. Of thoughts, imagination, ideas, and even dreams. And often the little one would wander off far away into these jungles, all alone. Radhika would worry as she sensed the distance and would struggle hard to pull her back. She knew that when Maulshree was disturbed by any idea or happening she could open the knots of her mind in front of her mother alone, reassured.

Often Maulshree would be lost somewhere sitting by herself. At such times her eyes would be focused on some point far away. When Radhika asked her what she was thinking about she would hesitate at first and then answer, 'I am not thinking, I am dreaming.'

'Dreaming? But you are awake!'

'But I am seeing a dream,' she would reply. Perhaps she had not yet understood the difference between thinking and dreaming. Nevertheless, Radhika's heart would fill with happiness on hearing her sweet and foolish, but unknowingly soaring, reply. What was this child of her like...slightly nutty!

The next instant Radhika would be unhappy. If she thinks so much, feels so much, she will be unhappy all her life, Radhika would think. After months and even years Maulshree hadn't forgotten that Kavita aunty had hurt her middle finger very badly when her hand had got caught in the door. She had lost track of all the happy moments spent with her aunt. When she met Kavita after a year, she asked her, 'Is your hand all right? Have you removed the bandage?' Even Kavita was surprised because she had almost forgotten the incident!

Amma had passed away a few months before Maulshree became three years old. Where has Amma gone suddenly? Why has she gone? When will she be back? Doesn't she miss me? There were many questions hovering around her for which she could not find the words. A story that Amma had gone away to the sky had been concocted to comfort her. 'She was very ill here, so God called her. Now she is comfortable there...' Her questions would stop on hearing this. She would get busy playing and everyone in the house would feel that her mind had been diverted. Radhika felt there was a constant waterfall of questions in her mind. The only difference was that the questions often became silent with the passage of time because even when they were spoken they were confronted with stories whose smell of insincerity even Maulshree could discern.

That year one day when the rains came for the first time marking the onset of monsoons, everyone sighed in relief at escaping the heat. The house was filled with the fragrance of wet earth and the kitchen was awaiting the smell of hot *pakoras*. Suddenly they heard the sound of crying. What had happened! Maulshree was standing in the courtyard crying loudly. Radhika went and hugged her, 'What is the matter, child...what happened?'

She was sobbing and only calmed down after a lot of cuddling. She said, 'My amma will get wet in the rain, she has forgotten her umbrella.'

Radhika was confused, 'But she isn't here, how will she get wet?'

'She is in the sky...the rain is coming from there,' Maulshree had said, sobbing, and it had taken nearly an hour to explain to her that the sky is above the clouds. The rain comes down from the clouds, it can't go up.

Those days Suhasini had come from Calcutta to visit them for a few days. Suhasini or Maulshree's Seemu Mausi or Seemu Mausu, who had changed the very fragrance of the house by her arrival. Maulshree had become the shadow of her Mausu who was dedicated to her *Rabindra sangeet*. To the extent that Amma's death had also become faint in her mind, though it hadn't been completely washed away. It used to flash through her mind occasionally, a fact that her Seemu Mausi had understood.

When Maulshree had happily worn the new frock brought by Seemu Mausi and stood in front of the mirror she had suddenly burst into tears. How would Amma be able to see her darling wearing this new frock? Then came the perpetual question, 'Will Amma never come back?' Mausu had taken on the task of comforting her and had explained in many ways that Amma would definitely return, not as Amma but as a little baby in some other house and added that 'this is the way it happens'. This idea sowed the seeds of another plant in Maulshree's mind. The next afternoon as she was putting her doll to sleep she asked her mother, 'Does everyone have to die?'

'Yes, child, but it isn't anything to fear or cry about.'

'Will you also die?'

'Yes.'

'And I?'

'Yes, but there is no need to think about all this now. You first have to grow up, go to school, college and do so many things.'

'Mausu says Amma has become a little baby. When you go to God, will you also become a little baby?' Another question had come up for which Radhika had no definite response and therefore she could just say, 'Yes.' But Maulshree had another question, 'Me too?'

'Yes.'

'But then I won't come back to this house. You won't be here. Amma isn't here, either,' Maulshree said.

'Yes, we will be in some other house,' Radhika wanted to end the discussion somehow. However Maulshree was close to tears, 'Then you won't be my mummy!' She was crying silently inside her heart. Radhika put her book aside and came close to her. Pushing all her logic aside she said, 'No, child, I will persuade God that he should make us mother and daughter. I will still be your mother.' Putting her face contentedly next to the edge of

Radhika's sari Maulshree was convinced that God would definitely listen to her mama.

And then a-year-and-a-half later came that night of 31 December when the atmosphere is full of hope, ready to welcome the New Year. A hope which touches the children as well. For the past two or three days Radhika had noticed that whenever Maulshree opened her casket it would include a few statements about the coming year and the bragging about some of her friends that they would be going out to dinner with their mummy-papa for New Year to some place where they would have a lot of fun at night. There would be dancing, singing, etc....

She would look questioningly at Mukul and Radhika as if to say that at least one of you should tell me what are we planning to do that night! Mukul's bald statement that 'We will cook something nice that night and watch the TV programme' did not meet with her approval. But nor did the four-year-old Maulshree had any other suggestions to offer to welcome the New Year. Radhika could understand the commotion in her mind but was silent. This was unbearable for Maulshree. Finally, she had to ask outrightly, 'Where will we go, Mama?'

'Nowhere' was Radhika's reply. She knew that it was not possible to keep any child completely away from consumerist values but she felt making the effort was worthwhile.

'Why won't we go anywhere? Everyone is going,' Maulshree asked pitifully.

'Just because everyone is going?'

'Let's go, Mama, please.' The fervent pleas had begun.

'No, child, what will we do there?'

'Then how will we celebrate the New Year?'

'Some other way.'

'But how?'

'Come on, let's think.' Radhika opened a realm of possibility before Maulshree.

'I don't know how to think,' a sulking voice replied.

'I will help you.' But Maulshree was upset. Radhika started the process of thinking, 'We will do something to help someone else, which will make others happy.'

'But how will we celebrate the New Year?' The needle was stuck at the same spot!

'Look, child, one can't talk when one is angry. First you get rid of your anger and then listen to me.'

'I am not angry any more,' Maulshree had said, still sulking.

'Do you know how much money we will spend if we go somewhere and sit there the whole night eating, dancing and listening to music?' Radhika continued the discussion, 'We will spend money but in a different way. For instance, just think that if we help someone with that money that person will be so happy and we will also get a lot of pleasure.' Maulshree was silent. Her little mind couldn't appreciate these idealistic statements.

'Look, it is so cold. Let's give some warm clothes to someone who is shivering with the cold. He will feel so good when he or she is nice and warm.'

'But how will we celebrate the New Year?'

Perhaps Maulshree wanted a straightforward reply to this question. Radhika was confused. How could she explain and make her understand? She couldn't even dream of spending the night in some expensive hotel with Maulshree. She wasn't willing to give up, 'Yesterday when we were returning from your aunt's place you looked at the men selling peanuts by the roadside and you had asked, "When are they going to go home? Aren't they feeling cold?" ' Now Maulshree could visualise the bundled-up peanut-sellers sitting in front of their little piles of peanuts. Radhika continued to speak, 'Do you remember I had said that they would only go home once they had sold all the peanuts?'

The questions in Maulshree's eyes were echoing in the silent room, 'So?'

Radhika drew closer to Maulshree and, stroking her back and shoulders, said, 'Why don't we go and buy all the peanuts from one of the peanut-sellers?' Maulshree couldn't understand but her eyes were filled with curiosity. She could see that Radhika was lost somewhere as she was speaking, 'Then that peanut-seller will go home and his children will be so happy that their father has come home early. Then they will all eat dinner with their papa. They will spend New Year's night together and their father will tell them a true story – a little girl came and waved her wand like a fairy. She gave me lots of money and bought all my peanuts...'

'What will his children say?' The thought had touched Maulshree.

'Anything. One of them will ask what this girl was like. Another will ask, "Did she have wings?" And yet another one will say, "She is a very good girl! I wish I could have seen her and made friends with her!" '

Many thoughts were floating through Maulshree's mind; she kept silent for a while. Then suddenly she came and pinched her mother's cheeks and clenched her teeth lovingly to show her affection as some indistinct words escaped her mouth, 'My Goofy, my love!'

And that night before dinner, shivering and bundled-up in a pile of clothes, mama and papa had taken their daughter to the market. There were some peanut-sellers scattered about the roadside. It was Maulshree's responsibility to decide whose peanuts were to be bought. She was walking ahead taking big strides, looking carefully at all the peanut-sellers. Mukul and Radhika were following her. Suddenly, Maulshree halted. She thought for a minute, then turned to her parents and said, 'We don't have to go any further. We will buy these peanuts.'

Radhika looked in her direction. There was an old woman selling peanuts. 'But her children will be quite old. They won't listen to any fairy tales.' Radhika was trying to undermine her choice.

'Doesn't matter! She must be feeling very cold.'

'Why?'

'Amma used to feel so cold! When I used to tease her about wearing a scarf like a child, she would say that children and old people feel very cold.' Radhika's heart was filled with warmth even on that cold night. They bought all the peanuts from the old woman.

After returning to home they ate dinner, chatted and watched TV for some time. But the atmosphere was filled with the warmth of that earlier moment, and it was this warmth which greeted the New Year.

Mama was Maulshree's ideal. She was the perfect woman whom Maulshree's little mind dreamt of emulating.

This was a dream which she cherished and nurtured. Her favourite diversion was to dress up in her mother's sari and high heels and walk around from one room to another. And sometimes if her mother indulged her daily request to wear some lipstick, Maulshree would really be on the seventh heaven! Lipstick was the most beautiful thing in the world for her. Often she would press her cheeks against her mother's lips affectionately and then giggle as Radhika's brows drew together in irritation at having her lipstick smudged. Sometimes she would try to touch her mother's lips with her tiny fingers and when she was reprimanded she would look at her with a helpless plea, 'Just a teeny-weeny, little bit.' And Radhika's annoyance would disappear.

Language and music were the most important things for Maulshree. Anyone associated with these two things could find a place in her heart. The yardstick which she used to test someone on the subject of language was her own name. If a person could not pronounce the word 'Maulshree' – the flower – correctly, he or she didn't deserve to be spoken to. When she met someone for the first time she would pay close attention to the way her name was pronounced by that person. It was the touchstone which determined whether someone deserved her friendship. Yes, those who learnt the right pronunciation after being corrected a few times could also be tolerated!

This personal whim of hers became a headache for the entire family when she obstinately insisted that Kamlabai should not enter the house. Initially no one paid much attention to her. This upset her even more. She took on the task of opposition single-handedly. When Kamlabai rang the bell, she would rush to the door and shout without opening it, 'The door is not going to open. It will never open. Go away. Don't come back here ever again.'

She refused to listen to any persuasion or arguments. She would be forcibly dragged away and the door would be opened somehow. This would offend her some more and then would begin the covert opposition against Kamlabai. Sometimes her broom would disappear, at other times mud would be put into the bucket of water she was using to swab the floor. If she couldn't think of anything else she would pull at Kamlabai's sari *pallu* as she was walking back and forth. The situation was deteriorating day by day.

If there was no one around, she would sometimes pull Kamlabai's plait and run away. When Kamlabai shouted and complained to Radhika, Maulshree would lose her temper completely.

She would respond to Radhika's attempts to calm her down by saying, 'She is dirty, throw her out. She calls me "Maulsree". Don't get mad at me when I call her Kamla not Kamlabai.'

Radhika was unable to explain to the young child why Kamlabai who was from Hathras was unable to pronounce her name correctly despite all her efforts. Finally she thought of a way to end the feud and decided that Kamlabai would now call Maulshree 'Gudiya'. But Maulshree could not allow this, she was only her Amma's 'Gudiya'.

In this situation Radhika had ultimately given Maulshree the responsibility of deciding an alternative name for herself which Kamlabai could pronounce correctly. This became quite a game for Maulshree. Often she would stand in Kamlabai's path and demand, 'What is my name, Kamlabai?'

'How would I know?'

Maulshree was reminded of her favourite resins, '*Kishmish*. Say *kishmish*.'

'What sort of name is this?'

'Yes, it is mine. Say it and I will let you go.'

Then Kamlabai would say '*kishmish*' and Maulshree would be delighted. The next day this '*kishmish*' would become some other dry fruit and yet another on the third. The only person in the world who was allowed to mispronounce her name was her Bajrang bhaiya. It was as though a cool dew drop fell on Maulshree when she heard him singing or humming a beautiful Nepalese melody as he walked around the garden taking care of the plants.

✦

Radhika also remembered the morning of the third of November. Maulshree was not yet two-and-a-half years old and she had been admitted to a small nursery school near the house. The reasons for sending her to school so early had been her loneliness and her desire to go to school. There she was looked after by Ira aunty and Mala aunty. The children were put under the supervision of different aunties depending on their age and temperaments. Some months slipped by quite happily. Every evening there would be a new poem, some mimicry, small incidents, new ideas, dreams, the unravelling of some thought and a tiny, lovely sunflower who bound all these together. But one day it became evident that the little flower was unhappy. There was no enthusiasm or excitement about the next day.

Maulshree had become quiet. She hated the thought of school. She had started turning somewhere inwards. She didn't enjoy going out of the house or playing with other children. When they enquired at school Ira aunty said that Maulshree had changed. She did not enjoy participating in any games and activities. She only wanted her mama. That was all. Many days passed like this. Radhika felt Maulshree had become very sensitive; she would cry very often and get irritated. Many attempts were made to discover the reason but without any success.

Radhika often explained to her that it was not good to be solitary and quiet. 'If we don't move around, meet new people, we will not learn new things. Then how will we grow? We will grow tall but remain stupid.' All the members of the family joined the campaign. Even Baba, her grandfather, was worried about his Gudiya's behaviour because she would go and hide in some corner of the house whenever any guest arrived and it would be difficult to find her. She was not willing to go to the market even when she was offered many temptations. When she was scolded she would compromise saying, 'I will go if mama is going.' She was teased by everyone including Radhika for being her mother's tail or mama's hangers-on. She hoped that this would force Maulshree to change her behaviour but nothing happened. All attempts to persuade her seemed to fail.

One of those nights mama and Maulshree were trying to sleep. The warm bed on a cold wintery night was enough to arouse Maulshree's hunger for a story. But that day she was unable to persuade her mother. Mama's eyes were too full of sleep after a hard day to pay attention to her demands.

'I won't tell you a story, I will sing a song. Keep your eyes closed.'

'I don't want to hear any horrible song. I want a story, a story, a story!'

'All right, let's pretend for today that I am your daughter and you are my mama. Now you tell me a story.' There was silence in the room. 'Come on, tell me a story, any kind of story.'

'You won't get angry, will you? Maulshree asked in a frightened voice and looked at her mother in the dim light as though she needed some reassurance. Radhika had somehow managed to say 'No' in a very sleepy voice. Again there was silence in the room. Radhika was going to sleep but Maulshree's eyes were swimming towards some unknown land. Suddenly, she started telling the story in a low voice:

There was a lipstick and a mirror. The lipstick was sitting quietly in front of the mirror. The mirror was upset when he looked at her. He said, 'Lipstick, what is the matter, why are you upset today?'

As the story progressed sleep vanished from Radhika's eyes. The strange story had shaken her up and she lay motionless, trying to read the emotions reflected on Maulshree's face. Maulshree's voice was gaining confidence as the story progressed.

The lipstick replied, 'Nothing.'

Mirror said, 'Say something, tell me more.'

The lipstick said, 'Just let me be, today I just feel like keeping quiet.'

'But what happened?' mirror asked again.

'Nothing at all,' she said.

Mirror spoke again, 'Look, you don't look good at all when you stay quiet and alone like this. Go and touch someone's lips, laugh a little, then you will look nice.'

'But I want to stay quiet just like this.'

'Don't say that. If you behave like this no one will talk to you. Powder won't speak to you nor will the cream and mummy's perfume.'

When lipstick continued to keep quiet, mirror felt very sad and he said affectionately, 'Dearest lipstick, good children don't behave like this. We look good only when we laugh, talk and play. If we keep quiet no one will love us. We will become bad.'

Then lipstick said, 'OK, since you insist I will listen to you.' It went off to decorate someone's lips and the mirror was very happy.

As the story came to an end Maulshree suddenly returned from her imaginary world to the present. The light in her tiny eyes disappeared and was replaced by an unknown fear – the fear of doing something unusual which one is unsure about. Like the apprehension which would precede a scolding from mama. But Radhika felt absolutely tender, partly because of happiness and partly because of her recognition of Maulshree's empathy. How much does this tiny three-year-old mind think! How deeply does she feel! Radhika gathered her close and started weaving her fingers through her curly hair. Curled around her mother, Maulshree lost that fear and gradually fell asleep. But now sleep had abandoned Radhika. She realised that the two protagonists of Maulshree's story were mother and daughter and Maulshree would only identify herself with the lipstick among the myriad objects that lay on the dressing table.

✦

The next day was unpredictable as though it was teasing the last few mornings. Preparations were being made to send Maulshree to school. Maulshree herself was a little quiet. That day she wasn't even refusing to go to school. Radhika was slowly untangling her hair when she asked softly, 'Mama, are you married?'

'Yes, child.'

'When were you married?'

'A long time ago, when you weren't around.'

'But you are still at home.' Radhika couldn't understand this question so she kept quiet. But Maulshree had decided to find her way out of one tiny jungle that day, 'You have to leave home after you get married.'

'Yes, I also left my home. Earlier I used to stay with your nana and nani. They are my parents.'

'Isn't this your house?' Radhika couldn't think of an appropriate answer to such a simple yet complicated question which a child could understand. She tried, 'That was my home earlier but after my marriage papa's home became my home.'

'Where was papa's home before he got married?' Another question confronted Radhika.

'This was papa's home even earlier.'

'Then why did yours change?'

'Because after marriage a girl has to change her home, not a boy.'

'Why?'

'That is the way it is. Now wear your shoes quickly, we are getting late.'

'When I get married this house won't be mine anymore?' Maulshree was still in the same world. Radhika couldn't think of any answer which was truthful but wouldn't hurt Maulshree's sentiments. Pretending not to hear the question she busied herself collecting Maulshree's tiffin, hanky and school bag. Maulshree said in a determined voice, 'I won't go to school. Never! It is a bad school. Mala aunty isn't there anymore. She will never come back. She has got married!'

The reasons for Maulshree's behaviour in the past few days had started revealing themselves. That day Maulshree did not go to school. Radhika did not insist and she also didn't go to work. She took Maulshree to Lodhi Garden. There both of them roamed around, enjoyed themselves, ate nice food, admired the flowers and chatted a lot. That afternoon discovered a new Maulshree – changed, happy, full of life.

✦

Was Maulshree really at peace with herself after that? And what could Radhika do about those eternal questions which would appear intermittently attached to some new incident or happening. She had managed to satisfy Maulshree that day but deep in her heart she knew that such questions which originated from the mounds of irony had mauled the psyche of countless people and continued to do so. These questions were everywhere – at every crossroad, at every corner, at every threshold, every doorway, under every roof; they even floated around in the air itself. They have become a part of our breaths. Should she stop breathing? But the question here was not about her. It was about that innocent, unmarked childhood which was knowingly or unknowingly being imprinted with these questions. Despite her efforts to hide them once in a while they would peep out at Maulshree. Actually, these questions were lurking around, hiding in some corner of her apparently happy and comfortable existence. Radhika could force them to stay quiet but did she have the ability to force them out of her existence? Within the boundaries of a joint family where extra courage was required to confront such questions? But she could not destroy the family arrangement just for this reason. How would Maulshree then have been able to experience the love and gentle affection of Amma and Baba? And then which other arrangement was perfect? She had decided that despite continuing to stay within the same arrangement, she would not allow her daughter's childhood to be dampened.

She had removed the thorn of Maulshree's statement – 'Boys don't have to cook!' – with Mukul's help. Amma was taken aback when one Sunday morning Mukul announced that he was going to make breakfast but Maulshree was even more surprised.

'Do you know how to cook?'

'*Arre*, wait and see what your papu knows! Ask Amma if anyone can make a better omlette than me!'

'Really?'

'Absolutely! Just see I will make a ball out of the omlette in the frying pan and I will even make it flip over.' Mukul answered waving his hands around and deepening his voice. Then the round omlette jumped and even landed safely on the frying pan. Many such Sundays followed after that day. Sometimes papu would even make Maggi for his 'cutie pie' in the evening. Then both of them would decorate the plate of noodles with *bindi*-like dots of sauce.

It was Mukul's love and support which had helped Radhika in her battle against these ironies. But where and to whom was she going to beg for help all the time! There were daughters in every household and they were all brought up like this. Her own life had also been based on such values. But there was something which troubled her, like a mote of dust in the eye. She wanted to save Maulshree's childhood from the same sense of discomfort. She wanted to protect its eyes from the dust and dirt. But how many times, and for how long?

One day a statement by Rajat had hurt Maulshree. Rajat had come over to her house to play. Maulshree happily told him, 'Let's go in and play *ghar-ghar*. You can be the papa and I will be mama. All the dolls will be our daughters.'

'I don't play with dolls. I am not a girl. I want to make a house with blocks.' They did play with blocks that day but Maulshree's thoughts continued to weave a complex web.

She could not digest Abhilekh's statement either that he wouldn't play cricket with her because girls weren't able to play the game. She thought about this statement for quite a while and then also came up with the question that why was it that only boys played cricket on TV.

Then one day she asked, 'Mama, if I had a brother wouldn't you have given me any milk to drink? Wouldn't you have let me play? Would you have only made me work?'

'Who told you all this ?'

'Nobody. I just know.'

'How do you know?' Radhika asked.

'I saw it on TV. All the mamas on TV do this,' she answered quite simply. Now Radhika had to explain to her that everything that happened on TV was just play-acting, it was not real.

She might have accepted this statement of her mother but how many such questions and discrepancies, which were invisible to the eye, continually spread their colours over her innocent, impressionable mind? All these discrepancies had gathered together, bonded together in her consciousness. That was why Maulshree's behaviour had suddenly become strange; a strangeness which revealed itself gradually. She had decided not to play with boys. She wouldn't sit next to them in the class. This problem became evident when one day at school she was asked to sit next to a boy instead of her favourite friend. She kept sobbing for an entire hour. When this happened again the next day aunty tried to figure out the reason for this behaviour. Maulshree replied, 'I won't sit next to any boy. I don't like boys.'

'Why don't you like them?'

'They are bad.' She didn't really have any reason to give.

✦

And then Radhika received another long letter from her aunty at school. A new problem. The entire family pitched in to find a solution. They tried to make her realise that both girls and boys were good. 'Boys who do bad things are bad just as girls who do bad things are bad. No boy or girl is bad just because he or she is a boy or a girl. Papa is a boy, Baba is a boy, uncle is a boy and they are all very good. They love Maulshree so much.' Efforts were made both at school and at home.

Maulshree cloaked her thoughts in such beautiful robes that it was impossible to gauge their depths even as one peeled off layer after layer. This was the reason why all these efforts to make her simpler and more childlike appeared to succeed at times whereas at other times they were unexpectedly unsuccessful. Sometimes it felt as though the knots in Maulshree's mind had been opened but on other occasions one realised how convoluted they were. And at such times Radhika would once again become disturbed and worried.

That day she had to go to Maulshree's school to talk to her teacher. Was she going to say that Maulshree had now become well-behaved, that she was just like other children? Discrepancies did not trouble her anymore, nor did they agitate her childish mind. Is that what Radhika wanted to hear? Perhaps! Perhaps not! She certainly wanted Maulshree to be happy, carefree, playful; she didn't want her to get lost in those moments which upset her and destroy her childish pleasures. But did she want her to lose that restlessness, that questioning mind which is the reality of the present, the energy which fuels struggle? The realisation which brings one person close to another, which opens one up to the sweet and sour experiences of life. No, definitely not! She knew that being Maulshree's mother she would always be called one day later or before for the PTA meetings. For one reason or another. She would continue her efforts to make Maulshree open up but as she unravelled one knot she knew there would be another knot replacing it. Finally it is these knots in her mind which will take Maulshree in some direction which provides a mirror for these ironies, she thought.

And Radhika got out of bed full of enthusiasm. She was supposed to visit Maulshree's school and that too a few days before the scheduled PTA meeting.

Hyphen

Some common misconceptions become such an intrinsic part of our lives that despite all reasons to the contrary, they continue to exist. For instance 'love-marriage' is a very common term. Often while using it a person or his pen is in such a hurry that the hyphen separating love from marriage is left out. And if someone does point out the omission one has to think hard to recall whether a hyphen really is required or not.

Gauri's visits to her aunt's house caused no less commotion than a mild earthquake. This was what Satyendra said and this statement had been repeated so many times in so many ways with so many different emotions that even Ragini now saw herself encountering that earthquake. That sweet, fragrant earthquake which bounced along like a tiny little ball was, in a sense, like Gauri's twin.

On her arrival the entire household, lying bundled-up in a silent corner, appeared to shake itself out of its stupor and stretch out in the lawn breathing in the fresh morning air. The soles of Ragini's feet would be surprised to find themselves taking in the morning dew which covers the grass but her mind soaked it up.

Gauri enjoyed dropping in, once or twice a week, at her aunt's place on her way back from college. Ragini felt she was almost like a bridge between the two houses. And then Gauri's arrival could mean a brief visit or an extended stay. The length of the stay depended either on Ragini's coaxing, or on Satyendra's offer to pick up some special treats on his way back from office. Pizzas or *kachoris*!

In Gauri's absence the memory of some incident or situation connected with her would follow Ragini around as she moved from one room to another, from the kitchen to the lobby or even outside on the lawn. Often when Gauri was casually narrating an incident or playing with little Manan, Ragini would look at her covertly and catch a glimpse of her brother in Gauri's glowing face. Time and circumstances could take a person so far away from loved ones despite their physical proximity!

Gauri was in class eighth or ninth when Ragini was married. After school when she joined college she started visiting her aunt's home once or twice a week because it was close to her college. The ringing of the door bell around two-thirty or three in the afternoon would fill Manan with a mischievous energy and Akka and Appa's faces would light up with anticipation. The expectation of another interesting afternoon and evening!

When did this period of three years begin and when did it come to an end! Then Gauri joined a French course which, by chance, was also near her aunt's house. Almost as though it was necessary for her to take admission only in an institution which was close to her aunt's house! So the string of enjoyable afternoons extended itself further.

Satyendra had gone to Bangalore on a tour for five days. There was a public holiday in the middle of this period. A holiday spent in Satyendra's absence was often very boring and uneventful. This awareness mingled with the morning tea filling the body with a leaden spirit. And then one had to get through the day somehow.

On one such morning Ragini felt her spirits rising when she found Gauri at the doorstep though she did wonder, for a moment, why Gauri had come over on a holiday and that too, early morning at eight o'clock.

She was once again filled with enthusiasm for making breakfast. Akka, Appa, Manan... everyone's limbs were filled with life and energy. Breakfast was a lot of fun despite Satyendra's absence. Leaving Gauri with Manan and Akka, Ragini started tidying away all the clothes which had been scattered about her room during the past week. Just then Gauri came in and sat down on the bed. Ragini looked at her curiously and smiled and asked, 'What happened?'

'Bua, papa is going to talk to you soon.'

'About what?'

'He... he wants me to marry Vijay Kaul's son.' Ragini looked back while putting the hangers in the almirah.

'And now you will say that you don't want to get married yet, isn't that so?'

There was embarrassment and irritation in Gauri's voice as she answered her, 'I do want to.'

Ragini was charmed and looked at her affectionately. 'Then get married.'

Gauri's ears reddened and she lowered her eyelids. She replied, almost pulling off the nail on the middle finger of her left hand, 'But not to him.'

'Then who? Is there anyone else?' Ragini exclaimed. She set aside the work she was doing and came and sat next to her. She took Gauri's hand in hers and looked at her face. Gauri had grown up! But when? The days have gone by so quickly, she thought. A question rang out, 'Tell me, Bua, should one have an arranged or a love-marriage?'

The rhythm of Ragini's heartbeats floundered. Love-marriage! Love! If there was a border line for love like the poverty line then…then one would realise how poor the world is. Three-fourths of the world would be below that line and the rest very close to it!

Stroking Gauri's hand Ragini fumbled for words, 'Where do you find love, my child…but if you do find it then you must value it.'

'But how?' Gauri burst out helplessly, 'Papa doesn't agree…and Boitoth is very angry. He hasn't spoken to me for two days or eaten a meal with me. He has shut himself away in his room.'

'But why? Who is this boy? He mustn't be a Kashmiri.'

'He is a Kashmiri…more than us…from Srinagar.'

'Then?'

'He is not a Pandit, his name is Shabbir…he is a Muslim.'

Ragini was stunned for a few seconds. Then she asked softly, 'Do you have faith in him…does he love you?' Gauri nodded her head in affirmative. 'But I am scared, Bua. I will leave everything for him but in case he changes, then?'

'This is true of every situation. If you marry someone of your father's choice, is there any guarantee that he won't change?' Ragini held her face and kissed her on the forehead. 'This is always a possibility, my dear. Move ahead with confidence…why should he change!'

Gauri's eyes were shining. She looked at her aunt, full of determination. That gaze heard her aunt saying, 'Look, we all need our space despite our need for a life-companion. If you have a love-marriage and you give that space to the other person, nothing will change. This space is necessary for the symphony of life, it is essential in every relationship. The closer you are, the more you will feel the lack of space.' Ragini was still thinking but her voice came to a halt.

She heard Gauri's voice, 'Bua, can I ask you something?'

Ragini's thoughts were scattered and she replied softly, 'Yes, ask.'

'Bua, you married someone of your own choice...against everyone's wishes, are you happy?'

A simple, straightforward question altered Ragini's chain of thoughts blurring her vision and she got surrounded by the blots. What answer could she give to this question? Could she just say 'yes' or 'no'? Perhaps. Perhaps not. Her breathing felt laboured and the reflection of the slackening of her heartbeat on her face made Gauri realise her mistake. 'Bua, can I make lunch for you today?'

✦

That day, after nearly nine years, Bansilal Mattoo's household had found itself at the same crossroads. Once again they were in a situation where he felt the need to lock himself away. But why? Why this time? Last time, nine years ago, when his daughter had announced her decision to marry the man of her choice, she had been as shaken as the rest of the household despite her determination. She was shaken because the man of her choice was a Maharashtrian, not a Kashmiri. How could the Mattoo family, which had spent the last forty-five years of its existence in an 'alien city' like Delhi clinging to the fragrance of the memories of its homeland Kashmir, accept this decision? Ragini's father, Boitoth, had taken a full month to approve of her choice. A suffocating month, with terrifying evenings and mornings which tried to hide their pain from the sunlight! An entire month spent in fear and apprehension.

Ragini had never resented Boitoth's anger. Despite the firmness of her own decision she could never say his anger was misplaced. There was as much justification for his anger as there was for her own firmness. It was also justified because it was Boitoth's anger. That Boitoth about whom Kakni used to say that he had fallen in love with a girl called Gulnaz when he was in college and it was his insistence to marry her which had been instrumental in sending him to Jammu, far away from Babuji. In the clash between the father and the son, Kakni had been pushed aside and left to heal the wounds of her heart.

Kakni said that Boitoth had got a job as a teacher in some school in Jammu and had decided to settle there. After six or seven months his maternal uncle persuaded him to come back to Srinagar. There he was quickly married off to Sukanya – the daughter of the Rainas – who lived in Baramullah. After this, Boitoth no longer wanted to stay in Srinagar. He came to Delhi with his wife and settled there permanently, and gradually life resumed its own rapid pace.

After a while Boitoth's younger brother also joined him in Delhi. He married a girl belonging to a Kashmiri Pandit family from Allahabad which had to sever their connection with their Kashmiri root and branch around 150 years ago. Although the daughter-in-law was a part of the family but the pang of the severed roots caused friction on both the sides. The atmosphere at home was dampened by the hide and seek of sweet and sour moments.

There was something which stayed alive in the recesses of the heart. An awareness which brought the chill of cool breezes, touched by the leaves of the *chinar*, to them even in this hot land! Otherwise why would Boitoth have explained to the nine-year-old Ragini one evening, 'Child, culture is very important. Remember this if you ever want to marry outside your community. You can marry a Kashmiri Muslim if you like, but don't marry a Madrasi or a Bengali just because you have the same religion as his. Our religion may be different but our culture, language and habits are the same. The joys of life will be the same.' And this day the same Boitoth was finding a Bengali or Madrasi Hindu more acceptable? How did religion manage to trample over culture? How do beliefs and ways of thinking change so much . . . or perhaps everything changes!

It was Kakni who, despite belonging to the eldest generation, explained to him that sometimes a father has to bow before the wishes of a grown-up daughter. She paused as she sat moving the prayer beads in her fingers and attempting to wipe out Boitoth's unhappiness she said, 'Everything will be fine once she gets married. How long can the rancour last?'

Ragini heard Boitoth's answer, 'Yes, but the ache remains.' Ragini felt his pain swell in her heart like the successive waves of rice terraces which notched the sides of the mountains. Sometimes when she looked into her being that moment still appeared to be frozen in place. A moment which almost shook her resolve. But she remembered Lalleshwari's dictum which she had heard from Kakni in her childhood that once you lose your soul your senses and mind keep searching for it fruitlessly for the rest of your life. Suppose she also lost her soul...But Ragini remained firm in her resolve...in the seventh heaven.

✦

'Ragini weds Satyendra.'

Ragini looked away after reading these three words on the invitation card. Setting it aside she leaned against the wall and closed her eyes. The words and the echo of their meaning kept reverberating through her being.

She slept for a brief while soothed by the echo and then she moved away, very gradually, leaving it behind her. When she opened her eyes she was surprised at how sometimes words could penetrate one's being visually and become a sweet song. Or, perhaps every word had its own music, a music which emerged from its context. Sometimes these melodies caused such a commotion that the mind became like a huge empty dome resonating with their echoes.

Satyendra's love had given her a feeling of spiritual comfort. Her life was so full of this affection that even contrasting, changing colours and fragrances had lost themselves in the collage of her life.

Relationships change and develop at their own pace, which is similar to the pace of life and time. Time – in which the present and the past intermingle and the future, unknown and unseen, also makes its appearance.

Ragini looked at these parallel movements without blinking. Satyendra was the high and the low note of her breath and her heartbeats. He was the uninterrupted melody which reverberated through the deepest caverns of her being. Then why had she surprised herself one day by unwittingly writing 'darkness/care of Satyendra Ranade' on a letter written to the void of life!

Why did Satyendra appear fragmented to her? The Satyendra whom she wanted completely had stepped into her life without any fetters, so why was it that now her very being cried out, 'These are merely small mercies.' Sometimes she could also sense a faint tension in the background. A lack of communication. A long wait for the layers of silence to disintegrate. Gazing, with the help of memories, at the reflection of a life which had come to a standstill. Finger prints on the face of time. The silent echoes of past days.

Ragini was a pure melody, vibrating to her own notes in the ups and downs of life. Taking care of school, home, family and everything, but remaining inviolate herself. But sometimes why did she feel as though Satyendra was an alien song!

✦

After years a morning filled with the fragrance of past moments had assumed the look of a sad evening. Ragini felt close to tears as she put down her cup after taking the last sip of tea.

'What are you thinking?' she asked Satyendra.

'Nothing…I mean nothing which concerns you.'

'Why not?' she spoke through her tears. 'I have been sitting next to you for the past fifteen minutes and you are lost in thoughts. You are not even looking at me…not even the barest touch…today is the day we…'

'Yes! But right now?'

'Is there a specific time for it? Where are you lost nowadays?'

'Ragi... Ragi... please... what has happened to you...?' Satyendra came closer and lifted her chin. 'Hey, you are a part of me, Ragini.'

Ragini rested her arms on Satyendra's shoulders and bent her head towards his heart. The grass was completely saturated with dew, 'Why don't you hold me close and say all this!'

Satyendra pulled her closer, putting his arms around her waist and said, 'You are crazy.'

Ragini knew that this was Satyendra, that he was like this. Still, why did she always want to hear him saying something even if it was excessively repetitious? Satyendra understood this and yet found himself unable to repeat all those words which she longed to hear. Perhaps he didn't think it necessary...or he didn't remember.

An insignificant matter becomes a big issue sometimes. Finally, love wiped away the dust of anger from Satyendra's face. And Ragini's sulking was not really annoyance! It was just a desire to be cajoled.

Ragini's lilting voice spread its glow, 'You will always remain a simpleton! Look, we have five senses, don't we? So what crime have our poor ears committed to be ignored? Don't they also want to be...' Satyendra's lips touched her ears, promising, 'We will take care of the ears as well, my sweet penguin.'

The whisper lost itself in their breathing and an ecstatic shiver flowed through her ears down to her innermost being...like a drop of mercury.

The three immortal words coined to express love in English sometimes became a philosophical conundrum for Satyendra.

Why does one need to repeat them again and again? Despite welcoming change and alteration at every step in life why do we continue to accept these words in their traditional form? And is it necessary to speak them out aloud? he thought. Ragini sometimes turned these very words into a question and placed them before him, just to irritate him. And all she wanted for an answer was 'yes'. A loud and clear 'yes' which others could hear but whose context they were unaware of. Sometimes, when the house was full of guests Satyendra would mischievously come close to Ragini and looking at her with a serious expression would say, 'Yes, Yes, absolutely!' Ragini would be taken aback. Satyendra would go away with the same expression on his face leaving Ragini stunned, feeling the sweetness of the words till the depths of her being. Then, for many days, the recollection of these moments would come back to her like a dream. Such moments were brief and rare, perhaps that was why they were so memorable. Why couldn't she accept this?

Warp and weft – two separate threads. Each completing the other and that is how a cloth is woven. Perhaps this difference is intrinsic to the primal relationship between man and woman and also its attraction.

✦

'Hello Ragi... Satyendra here!'

'Yes, Satyendra, how are you?'

'Absolutely fine... listen, has Akka's report arrived?'

'Yes, there is nothing to worry about, all is well.'

'Where is Manan? Can he talk?'

'He has gone out to play... is your work over?'

'Yes, first class! I have bought your sari, the same colour, your favourite pink.'

'Oh, Satyendra, really? Hello...hello...I can't hear you, speak up.'

'Nothing much...I am coming back tomorrow.'

'And...?'

'By the afternoon flight.'

'And...?'

'And...and what you want to hear, take care, bye.'

The entire night and the next day those unspoken words embellished her dreams till the moment of Satyendra's arrival in the evening. An evening whose misty light handed over the perfumed garland of darkness to the night waiting around the corner.

The entire household was cocooned in that darkness. Ragini would peep out at the flowers once in a while. The drowsiness of sleep hovering on the threshold of her eyes suddenly spied a smiling little dream. It had drawn the dream close by its warm little hand. Slowly, slowly, so that her eyelids would not be startled! But the dream would not be controlled despite its diminutive size and Ragini's eyelids snapped open and woke her up. Enfolding herself within the sound of Satyendra's warm breathing in deep sleep, Ragini spent that cold night in the world of intimacy. Warming herself with those moments.

Hearing the chirping of birds she reached up to the curtains and moved them aside. Outside, night and day were almost at the point when they meet. The gentle breeze was conversing with the flower-laden branches of the bottle brush growing in front. The branches swayed in one direction or the other trying to hide their smiles as they listened to the breeze. Outside the window, the queen of the night was intoxicated by the perfume of its own white flowers. Satyendra's breath snagged as he woke up. The perfume had really become intoxicating. The breeze swept past Satyendra saying, 'I wish there was a deep pool filled with love and you would drown me in it, push me in whenever I raise my head... if I raise my head... if I shout that I am suffocating... please don't listen to me...'

Tangible moments carried an intangible warmth down to the deepest layers of Satyendra's bone marrow. The flow of breath was sweeping Satyendra towards a new creation. Life was replete.

Gauri had asked Ragini a question. Its reply could only be another question asked by Ragini.

Life needs momentum. And as it races along, it takes warmth from the burning bushes of passions. No moment is willing to rest and stop! Who... who will understand that passions are like burning incense? They become smoke in order to perfume homes and minds of people. Incense cannot make the whole world fragrant... Its fragrance cannot travel too far but it leaves its impression which inhabits the mind. Should that perfume be wiped out?

Perhaps love-marriage is a similar fragrance. There are too many expectations from it. Expectations which are very dear to us, like a brand new car which we love with our heart and soul, which we care about, which we are proud of... and expectations from an arranged marriage are like a second-hand car which we first accept with detachment and reluctance but we gradually get used to it. We get so used to it that merely the sound of the engine can tell us if there is a problem.

Perhaps both kinds of marriage ultimately arrive at the same destination. On the way sorrow, pain, disappointments constantly carpet the path. The quantum of pain in life is proportionate to the degree of love. The wheels of life drive on this path of pain which is interspersed by big and small joys. It is possible that happiness comes merely to break the monotony of sorrow. To give space for a breather. To provide some change. And then it depends on our nature how often we open the folds of pain and look at them before putting them away. Life will show wear and tear if it is used. Perhaps life doesn't become just a sleepless prelude in a love-marriage... that is if one preserves the meaning of these two words retaining the hyphen in between. There is a rule which was followed in the construction of old buildings. The walls were not made of a single layer of bricks; they were double-layered with a gap in between to insulate the building against heat and cold.

Why is it that after a while, in a love-marriage, it is only love which matters to a woman and marriage which is important to a man? Both of them, however, often miss the hyphen.

✦

On her return from school Akka told her that Gauri had come. That day she chatted even more than usual. She was looking very happy and lovelier. In the afternoon Akka and Appa went to their room to rest. Manan also went with them, so Ragini decided to go to her room. She decided to correct some copies to keep herself relatively free at night. She picked up the copies and a red pen and started to work on them. While she was working her gaze suddenly fell on the table in front of her where a piece of paper, wedged with a paper weight on top of some books, was fluttering in the breeze. She rose, picked up the scrap of paper from the table and started to read:

Bua,
I have taken a decision and I am going to tell the family today. I am going to marry Shabbir. A love marriage. I hope you are happy.
Love,
Gauri

While reading the paper Ragini pulled out the ball pen which she had pushed into her hair bun and absent-mindedly put a hyphen between the words 'love' and 'marriage'. Putting the paper back on the table she shoved the pen back into her hair. As she walked from the bed to the table, the edge of her sari moved the rocking chair placed in between, and it rocked back and forth gently. Ragini stopped for a moment and looked at the chair. Then, sitting down in the chair, she removed the pen and clip from her hair so that it unwound itself and spread out freely over her shoulders. She closed her eyes. The warmth of a smile followed the faint glow in her eyes. Ragini felt as though she had been very tired for long and now that tiredness was leaving her; slowly, slowly. She pushed the chair a little to increase its movement and let herself flow along with its rhythm.

Saplings of Fear

'*Arre*, she died longing for a grandson, such a meaningless life. God, what have you done... I will go to hell now... I couldn't even give her a grandson... she won't climb the golden stairs of heaven... oh!' Sudha's ears were ringing with the screams coming from the folds of the grimy sari covering the head of the woman sitting in the tiny room. A room stuffed with fifteen or twenty women where a thirty-year-old mother of four daughters was lamenting the death of her eighty-year-old mother-in-law. Three of her tiny, grubby and frightened-looking daughters were watching this scene, wide-eyed. Outside, in the courtyard, a crowd of men had gathered who were making preparations to take away the dead body. Intermittently, from the tiny room, came the lamentations of the daughter-in-law that despite having three sons and daughters-in-law, the old lady's hope of having a grandson had remained unfulfilled. Being jostled around in the DTC bus, Sudha constantly pushed back the memory of this scene but somehow it intruded into her consciousness creeping in from different directions. '*Arre*... my life has been worthless despite giving birth to four...'

'Is there anyone for Yusuf Sarai . . .?' Suddenly, she heard the voice of the conductor. Then the bell rang and the bus moved forward. Sudha stood up hastily. She had to get down at the next stop. She had thought she would buy some vegetables in Yusuf Sarai before going home but she had passed it. By the time she was pulled out of her thoughts, it was already too late.

Getting down from the bus, Sudha walked home but the lament continued to follow her. Even in the bus she had shaken herself and looked out of the window but she had seen the same lament outside the window. She understood that it was not going to be easy to shake it off. It would accompany her home that day.

The woman with the crushed sari was Badri Srivastav's wife. Badri worked as an assistant editor in her office. Hearing about the sudden demise of his mother in the morning, many people from the office had gone in official vehicles to his house to offer condolences. Sudha had visited the house for the first time. In the office her interaction with Badri Srivastav was very limited and sparse. But she could never have imagined that every brick in the home of a man who worked as an assistant editor would be dyed in the colours of age-old customs. Despite so much education, the breath of new ideas and thoughts had not even skimmed the surface of those tradition-bound bricks. Even at a time when there was a dead body lying in the house, Badri's wife was saddened more by her inability to give birth to a son, by the fact that she could not fulfil her mother-in-law's desire for a grandson. She was upset that she had given birth to four daughters, though one of them had died as soon as she was born. She felt that because of this deficiency she had never become a wife, daughter-in-law, or even a mother in the true sense.

After crossing the road in front of Green Park market and taking the right turn into the first lane Sudha's house was the third in the row. She took a deep breath before ringing the bell, visualising the scene inside. Suddenly a voice called out, 'The door is open.' Sudha walked in feeling a little foolish. In the drawing room Bahua, her mother-in-law, was sitting on the divan sorting out fenugreek and spinach greens which were spread out on a newspaper. Sudha gave a faint smile and walked through the drawing room towards her own room. 'I was waiting for you till now…then I thought I might as well sort out the vegetables. I just had my tea, my cup is still lying here.'

Sudha knew that Bahua had not uttered even a single word which was objectionable but each of her words felt as though it was weighing Sudha down. Whenever she was late from work Bahua's words would have the same impact on her. They reminded her that once again she had neglected her home for the world outside. Her external life was once again encroaching on her life inside the house.

Sudha went inside without giving any reply. She had a bath and then glanced at the kitchen. A neat and clean, well-ordered kitchen. She knew that this was not merely a kitchen but an extension of Bahua's existence which she wanted to pass on to Sudha. But Sudha was not bothered about this. She refused to be limited merely to a kitchen. She had no specific aversion to it but she had no intention of dedicating her life to it, either. She recalled how much the appearance of the kitchen had changed. Around twelve years ago its focal point was a *thali* – Babuji's *thali*. The afternoon *thali* and the evening *thali*. That *thali* was the raison d'etre not only of the kitchen but of Bahua herself. She existed because of it. Bahua's daily routine and even Sudha's, to some extent, revolved around that *thali*. It was the axis of the kitchen. At that time the fire in the kitchen was never put out during daytime, almost as though it was competing with the sun!

The *angithi* was lit at six in the morning and was only allowed to cool down at six in the evening. It was the kitchen which symbolised the honour and respectability of a house and what was the use of kitchen with a cold stove! Chotu fed the fire every few hours by putting in fresh coal. Bahua constantly kept placing different utensils on the fire; if the tea was made then the vegetables had to be cooked; if the rice and lentils were ready then warm rotis needed to be prepared. If there was nothing left to do then at least one could boil some potatoes or just heat some water. It always came in handy. The stove should not be unoccupied. One was so busy reigniting the coal fire after every use and keeping the *angithi* occupied that one didn't even notice the silent arrival of the night!

No one spared the thought that the new daughter-in-law, who had a master's degree in English, might want to peep outside the kitchen. At times she would get upset with this arrangement. Once she gathered enough courage to suggest that the gas stove in the kitchen could be used for other things apart from making tea and rotis and that the use of the coal fire could be coordinated more efficiently to free them from the kitchen more quickly. Bahua had listened to her suggestion very calmly and then asked, 'What will we do then?' Sudha tried to explain that they could read some books or magazines in the free time. The answer was, 'Books are read by those who have nothing to do. There is no shortage of work in the house! You begin something small and then realise how much more work remains to be done.' Sudha felt quite small.

She did not have the courage to speak to Babuji. She barely spoke to him throughout the day. And then when she remembered the affectionate instructions she had got from him a few weeks after her marriage, she often looked at each of her decisions and actions with scepticism. 'Is this correct or wrong?' 'Does it fit into the code of conduct defined for a good daughter-in-law?' This feeling of inadequacy had been with her ever since that day.

She remembered that Yogesh had come to Delhi for work a few weeks after her marriage. One day they had invited him to dinner at home. They chatted so long into the night that everyone asked him to stay on for the night. In the morning Sudha was ironing his shirt so that it would be neat enough for office and he was standing next to her chatting when a voice came out of Babuji's room, 'Anyone can iron the shirt, Daughter-in-law, why don't you go and help Bahua in the kitchen?' There was something in the tenor of the voice which halted not only her hands but her laughter, too. There was a wealth of meaning in those words which she was unable to decipher accurately at that moment. Yogesh took the iron from her saying that he would iron the shirt himself, after all he did it everyday. Sudha went into the kitchen to help Bahua. The atmosphere was very easy and informal till the afternoon. Yogesh was sent off very cordially. Everyone had their lunch and then went up to the roof to welcome the gentle warmth of the winter sunshine.

Suddenly Babuji called her into his room. A resolute and sober voice touched her ears, 'You are now the daughter-in-law of the house. You should not laugh and joke around with men who are strangers. This is not proper.'

'But Yogesh is not a stranger, Babuji.'

'I know, but he is not your real brother, is he?'

She had not said another word. She stood with her eyes downcast. Babuji thought all this about Yogesh! Her maternal cousin! Yogesh was three years older to her but when they used to fight in childhood it was she who often had the upper hand. And she had never thought of him as anyone else than a brother. She had spent months and years with him. And today Babuji is having such thoughts! she thought. She suddenly felt she had become a daughter-in-law. She had to think before every step she took. Even before laughing. There was a new code of conduct for her with which she was not yet familiar. And that day a part of her ceased to exist.

A few weeks later there was a letter from Sajjo from Benaras. It filled the house, and especially Bahua's life, with happiness. Sajjo mausi, Bahua's youngest sister, was going to be blessed with a child after fifteen years of marriage. How was it possible for Bahua not to visit Benaras on such an occasion? And then she could now think about leaving the house for a few days. It was easier to place the request before Babuji because now there was someone who could look after the house. The house and the kitchen. And the *angithi*!

Bahua had managed to go only for a few days. One day Sudha was sitting at the dining table eating a meal with Babuji and Rohit. When she offered Babuji a bowl with *gulab jamuns*, he said, 'What is the matter? We are having both carrot *halwa* and *gulab jamuns* today!' Babuji had changed a little after Bahua's departure. There was less tension in the air. Not because Bahua was the cause of any tension but because he did not feel as much at ease in her absence. He was conscious of his strict personality, so he tried to be softer when she wasn't around.

Rohit answered enthusiastically, 'You will have to eat these, after all we have completed a hundred days of marriage today.' Sudha felt a little uncomfortable. She kept her gaze on the *pulao* in her plate.

'A hundred days! Then this is truly a very significant day…'

Rohit was very happy but Sudha felt those words had a different meaning. Perhaps she sensed sarcasm in those words. She became a little careful. She felt something more was still to come.

'So what did you do today?' Babuji said, smiling in an attempt to behave naturally. Rohit kept chatting in his enthusiasm, 'Nothing special. We just went to the market in the evening. We roamed around for a while and bought these *gulab jamuns* on our way back, thinking that we should share this day with everyone at home and then…' But Babuji was somewhere far away. Sudha was still trying to make sense of Babuji's earlier statement. While thinking she pushed a spoon of *pulao* into her mouth so that Babuji wouldn't realise that she was trying to understand him and figure out the real meaning of his words.

'Yes, but today is a very important day. You have completed hundred days of marriage. This day is actually a milestone!' Each word of Babuji was very pointed and direct, 'Today you and especially Sudha should think about what you have lost and gained.' She was shrinking inside herself. An invisible fear had reddened her ears and her face. Babuji continued, 'I meant what did you do during these days which was correct and what wrong things you did.' Sudha saw black spots in her plate. The bowl of *gulab jamun* became misty and blurred.

'You should look back and think to what extent you have imbibed the traditions and customs of this house and how much you still need to do. A hundred days are more than enough for a daughter-in-law to mould herself according to her new home.' By this time Rohit had also sensed the difference in the atmosphere. The room was completely silent with only Babuji's voice echoing in it, 'For instance, let us talk about the morning. You greet me every morning with a *namaste*. Good! But by now you should have realised the custom of this house. *Namaste* is fine but it isn't enough to say the word and barely shake your head. I have never been able to understand what this nodding is. A daughter-in-law doesn't say *namaste*, she does *pranam*.' His voice had gradually hardened, 'Doing *pranam* is a tradition. It may not tally with English literature but a home is a home, not the world of literature.' Sudha had somehow managed to swallow her dinner. That day would often flash through her mind. Rohit had tried very hard to calm her down but finally he had given up, exhausted, and spent the rest of the night counting the rings in the ceiling.

She did not know how five years of her marriage passed by interspersed with innumerable such incidents. Then, there came a ray of hope, something to break the monotony and loneliness of the house and her own life. On a beautiful spring day her breaths and her unbearable pain had welcomed Asavari into the world.

When she came home from the nursing home she found that the entire room was perfumed with the smell of narcissi. Rohit's love. Always silent, quiet and yet expressing so much, conveying meaning without words. In the evening Bahua had asked Rohit, 'What should we name our little doll?' She had involuntarily interrupted, 'Asavari' and then felt a little embarrassed by her impatience. The next instant her mind was occupied with the thought that she may not have been able to learn music properly, yet at least a raga would play in the courtyard of her life and perfume every corner of her house with its sound. Everyday she would embellish, love and beautify that raga. . . .

Bahua and Babuji did not like this unusual name. They even expressed their disagreement a few times to Rohit but his determined silence finally defeated them. Rohit knew that Asavari was Sudha's dream, a very cherished and personal dream. This time he kept quiet to support Sudha. In any case he did not like confrontations.

✦

'Make some tea for Rohit as well, I think he has also come home.' Sudha was startled when Bahua called out from the drawing room. Pushing aside all thoughts of the past she glanced at the saucepan. After putting the tea on to boil she walked into the drawing room and discovered that Bahua had almost finished sorting the fenugreek and the spinach. 'Should I take this away?' she asked. Dusting her hands Bahua said, 'Take it, I have chopped it and kept it ready, now it is up to you. If you want you can cook it now or in the morning.' She had picked up the *thali* of greens and moved towards the kitchen when Bahua said, 'Asavari said she doesn't want to eat any greens...make some potato curry for the two of us. I and my granddaughter don't like these green vegetables of yours...give me some potatoes, I will cut them for you.'

The water for tea had boiled. Rohit arrived as soon as the tea was ready. While everyone was having their tea, Asavari returned from music school. The father and daughter started their usual discussions and chatter which Bahua and Sudha enjoyed every evening. But that day this commotion seemed strange because behind it was the shadow of the lament which had been issued from behind the veil.

The entire house came to life with Asavari's arrival. She had brought this laughter with her when she was born. Babuji had also melted a little after her arrival. When the baby Asavari lovingly lisped his name 'Babu', a gentle tenderness could be glimpsed behind the stern look on his face. Yes, Bahua and Babuji did hope that Asavari would not be the only child. She should have a brother though they realised that it was better to wait for a few years. Babuji, however, could not wait so long. He passed away when Asavari was merely two years old. Bahua never spoke about her secret wish because she understood her son's temperament. In the meantime Sudha had started working as a sub-editor in a government organisation.

As Asavari grew up Sudha wanted to give her every opportunity to develop her personality. Even those opportunities which she herself had been denied or had missed. She wanted to become a dancer but she was taken out of dance school when she was in the seventh class because Baba believed that girls from decent families did not perform on stage. She did B.A. in economics after schooling and then she wanted to do business management. However, she got admission outside Delhi and because of this she had to let go of the opportunity. A girl, after all, could not be allowed to stay away from home for two years. She expended her anger on economics by saying goodbye to it and switching to literature for her master's degree. It was only after studying literature that she had truly understood relationships between one human being and another and between men and women. She realised that all those things around her which caused her pain, which made her feel small and diminished, which made her feel helpless and which were invariably supported by her parents were not merely a part of her life but, beyond differences of place, history, language, they were present in every aspect of society. The lament from behind the veil started echoing once again, 'I will go to hell…I couldn't become a mother despite giving birth to four…I couldn't give her a grandson.'

Sudha had also cried once after Asavari's birth. Not because her child was a daughter and not a son but at the thought that her daughter would also have to face the same discriminations and dissonances at every bend in her life. There would be many such moments in her life when despite her education and financial independence, she would find herself helpless. Saplings of fear with innumerable faces will sprout in her mind and she will be forced to live with them and nurture them day and night. The lament insidiously crept in and spread through the entire house like smoke. '…*Arre*, she died without fulfilling her hope of a grandson, her life, this birth was worthless…'

Offerings of Memories

A bulldog chews a bare bone for hours knowing that there is not even a fragment of meat attached to it. It continues to enjoy its flavour. It is because of this habit of the dog that fake bones are now available in the market. If nothing else, at least these fake bones give the illusion of being real bones!

Kakni lay almost supine on the cane chair in the verandah, lost in her thoughts as usual. Who knows which knots of life she was busy unravelling! Having reached almost the age of ninety, I wonder what she thinks about all the time, Shakti thought to herself, looking through the window towards the verandah. Ninety years! Her grandmother, Kakni, was now almost ninety years old.

Suddenly Shakti was struck by the thought that Kakni's legs must be tired after hanging down for such a long time. Picking up a low stool, she came out and gently placed Kakni's legs on it. Kakni twisted her neck, threw a listless glance at Shakti, and rested her head on the chair once again. She continued to gaze at the street outside with the same look. Maybe this helps her to pass the time! With this thought Shakti stroked her grandmother's hair affectionately. I am seeing you after three years... I wonder if I will be able to see you next time I come! Shakti thought to herself. As she reached out to pull down the maxi which had ridden up Kakni's legs, she recalled the days when her family, like so many of their relatives, saved themselves from the conflagration of exile in Srinagar and somehow took refuge in Jammu. Till that time Kakni used to wear a *pheran,* and on her head she would wear either a kerchief or a *taranga* – the traditional head dress of Hindu Kashmiri women.

A long time before Independence, the social reformer Kashyap Bandhu had exhorted Kashmiri women to give up the old-fashioned *pheran* and adopt the sari. His reformist call had such an impact that *pherans* had been banished overnight and stored away in huge trunks kept in the attics of all the homes. Only the older women were left amazed, watching the progress of this procession of change from their windows. They did not try to stop the younger women of their households, but encouraged them instead. Kakni was a young woman at that time. She also liked saris but she could never forsake her beloved *pheran* for it. Even the whirlwind of change raging around her and Kashyap Bandhu's call could not change her mind. But the difficult times they faced after banishment and the heat in Jammu had shaken her. In Srinagar she had refused to change her mind despite having arguments with her son Kashinath but on their arrival in Jammu she told him one afternoon, 'I was thinking that I should give up my *pheran*. When I have lost everything that I spent my entire lifetime gathering, why should I continue to carry the burden of this attachment...?'

Realising her state of mind Kashinath tried to console her, 'Now that you have worn it till today...'

'I did a lot of things till today, accumulated so much…it was all an illusion…then…' she interrupted him, 'it will be difficult for me to learn how to tie a sari at this age…and where do I have to go…'

'Then what…'

Kakni interrupted him once again. This time deliberately because she realised that his words were going to weigh heavy on the tears that she was holding back, 'Nothing. I will ask my daughter-in-law to give me one of her maxis and I will wear a dupatta instead of the *taranga* on my head.' And thus, Kakni turned her face away from the Kashmiri dress which had been passed down to her by generations of her ancestors.

Kakni suddenly sat up when Shakti tugged her maxi down towards her feet. 'What happened, Kakni?' Shakti asked her, alarmed.

'Arundhati…Arundhati…' Kakni called out, looking towards the street as she took her feet off the stool and placed them on the ground.

'What is the matter, Kakni…who is Arundhati?'

'That is Arundhati, stop her…' She gathered her strength and called out, 'Arundhati! Arundhati…where are you going?'

Shakti's mother rushed out on hearing Kakni's voice, 'What happened to Kakni?'

'I don't know…she is calling out to someone.' Shakti tried to support Kakni by offering her a shoulder but Kakni was suddenly infused with such tremendous energy that she pushed Shakti's hand aside and told her daughter-in-law, 'Bahu, look, Arundhati is going…stop her…'

'Which Arundhati?'

'*Arre,* the one from Badgaam...just call out to her, otherwise she will go away.'

In a rather irritated tone Ma told Shakti, 'Shakti, take her in...she is not feeling well.'

'Ma, she becomes a little strange when she is inside...let her stay here awhile...'

'It will be difficult for us to live even in this place if she starts calling out to women walking by on the street. Take her in...'

Before Shakti could move ahead to help her Kakni stood up on her shaky legs and started walking towards the gate. Shakti rushed ahead to support her and with her help Kakni reached the gate and called out once again, 'Arundhati! Arundhati!' On hearing her voice, an elderly woman who had walked ahead a few steps looked back. Kakni's eyes shone with an innocent joy, 'Arundhati...how are you? What are you doing here?' When the elderly woman with salt and pepper hair, wearing a printed sari came towards the gate, Ma also came forward, looking harassed. 'Listen, please don't pay attention to her...actually...she is quite old.'

'But she isn't wrong, I *am* Arundhati.' Ma was stupefied on hearing the old woman's reply. Words crowded in her mouth, almost as though they were trying to hide behind each other.

'Open the gate, bahu...Arundhati will come in.'

Ma was surprised at first but then she opened the gate and Arundhati walked in a little uncertainly but with some curiosity. Ma gestured towards a chair and said, 'Please sit down.'

'Wait, first I must embrace her...we are meeting after so many years.' On hearing Kakni's words, Arundhati came forward and embraced her. Shakti helped Kakni to sit on the chair once again, 'Kakni, sit down and chat.' When Arundhati had also sat down,

Kakni said, 'Bahu, make some tea, Arundhati has visited us after a long time.' Ma walked towards the kitchen a little reluctantly.

'But please forgive me...I don't remember you,' Arundhati said.

'*Arre,* you don't recognise me, Arundhati?...I was your eldest sister's closest friend...Kala...Kalavati.'

'Kalavati?'

'You have forgotten? What is this world coming to! This is *Kaliyug*...I am so old and I can remember everything but you don't remember anything!'

'I am not too young, either. I am going to be seventy-five...how much can I remember in this old age!'

Kakni said, '*Arre,* Arundhati, didn't your sister live behind the Ganpatyar temple? And my house was in the lane behind which was the street where her house was located. Do you remember now? Your sister Sharda...may God give her a place in heaven...she left two small children behind when she passed away at such a young age. Perhaps it was for the best, after all what is there in this world to live for!'

Arundhati was looking at Kakni, astonished, knocking at the doors of her own memories.

'*Arre,* you can forget me but how can I possibly forget you! You are the one who taught me how to cook lentils with radish. Whenever Kashinath's father praised the dish after a meal, I used to remember you. Whenever you visited your sister you would cook something new. You were the one who taught me to cook *chana dal* with spicy *vadis*. I think you learnt it from some Punjabi tourist. I used to wait for your visits..."When will Arundhati come?" I used to keep asking Sharda.' Kakni suddenly wiped her eyes with the dupatta hanging around her neck. 'Once Sharda passed away I did not feel like going anywhere near her house or even the lane where she lived. She was a very good person... more than a mother to you... you were her life.'

Arundhati could not recollect anything. Hesitantly she said, 'You are right.'

Kakni said, 'Sharda was the eldest daughter and also the eldest daughter-in-law. She was burdened with responsibilities from both sides. On the one hand she would worry about her motherless brothers and sisters and on the other hand she had to deal with useless brothers-in-law and fiendish sisters-in-law. Sometimes she would try to lighten her heart by recalling the Persian saying her grandfather often used to repeat – "*Buz baash buzurg ma baash*", which meant that it is better to be a bearded goat which is soon going to be slaughtered rather than being an elder!'

The constant knocking on the doors of Arundhati's consciousness finally bore fruit. A dark room full of cobwebs at the back of her mind was suddenly illuminated. 'Yes, whenever she said this to us we would tease her saying elders always have a good time, they can do what they like, eat what they like. No restrictions! And then we would add the next line of this Persian saying – "*Sag baash khurd ma baash*", which meant that it is better to be a dog on the doorstep, wagging your tail, rather than being the youngest in the house!'

'Oh, wonderful, I didn't know this part.' Kakni excitedly repeated the line once more, '*Sag baash khurd ma baash... sag baash khurd ma baash!*'

'What a time that was!' Arundhati said, laughing, and Kakni agreed with her happily. The verandah echoed with their combined laughter as Ma and Shakti watched amazed.

'Tell me did that wicked mother-in-law of yours finally give the house to you and your husband, or did she leave everything to her beloved son? She was your husband's stepmother, wasn't she? How she used to trouble you, the horrible woman!'

'Kakni... Kakni, what are you saying! Shakti interrupted worriedly and said to Arundhati, 'Please don't mind her words.'

'How can I be upset, child... one can't be offended by the truth,' Arundhati said.

'You have no idea how much this poor woman has suffered,' Kakni told Shakti, 'her sister Sharda used to weep when she would talk about her difficulties... and who could she share her sorrows with.' Then Kakni turned to Arundhati, 'Your mother had passed away when you were very young. *Arre,* that mother-in-law of yours... '

Arundhati interrupted, 'Let's forget about her. These are all old stories... I was destined to bear these sorrows. Whatever she was like, she is now in another world... what is the point of criticising her!'

'Yes, you are right. Tell me, where have you come from?'

Ma entered just then with the tray of tea and Shakti picked up a cup and passed it to Arundhati.

'You know we lived in Badgaam. Something strange has happened to him ever since we came here.'

'Who? Your husband? What has happened to him?' Kakni asked, leaning forward.

No, no... God forbid! Nothing should happen to him. But he hasn't been able to forget his home... his city. Once we came here all he did was, cut out news items about Kashmir from the newspapers and collect them. He would cut them, collect them in a file... God knows what he would do. There were masses of files full of these news items and photographs. They would be covered in dust but no one could touch them even to clean them. The children longed to hear different programmes on the radio but he wouldn't permit anyone to shift its needle from "Radio Kashmir".'

'Where is he now?' Ma asked in a sympathetic tone.

'Where will he go! He is very much here…at least he was here till last week but…'

'But?' Shakti asked inadvertently.

'Last week he left home in the morning saying he was going to the temple…'

'Then?' Ma was losing her patience.

'Then I don't know…he hasn't returned. What could we do? We lodged a report with the police. It was of no use…but day before yesterday our neighbour, Tanvir Riyaz, called from Badgaam. He said he saw a shadow in our locked house. He went to check…and it was my husband. Who knows why he left without telling anyone!' Arundhati hid her face in the corner of her sari as she spoke and started sobbing.

Ma went close to her and tried to console her, 'Now at least you know where he is…he will come back soon.'

'Yes, he will come back…what do we have left there except four lifeless walls and a pile of debris.'

'Debris!' Shakti exclaimed.

'It is debris if it is of no use to us…now his food is sent to him from Tanvir's house. He was telling us that my husband refuses to leave the house even for an instant. He keeps opening the trunks, airing the clothes and putting them back…he cleans all our things and puts them back in place. That is all he does the whole day…' Arundhati started crying in earnest.

'You are really unlucky. First your mother-in-law didn't let you live in peace, and now your husband!'

'Kakni, please!' Shakti interrupted her.

But suddenly Ma supported Kakni, 'It isn't just her bad luck, all of us are unfortunate, otherwise why would we be wandering around so far from home!'

'You are right, bahu. It is really difficult to live through these interminable days. There we lived in our own neighbourhood, among our own people. Here we just wait for the sun to rise and set.'

Then Arundhati said, collecting herself, 'We had got used to life... and now this new headache! One of his friends, Shiv Lal Bhan, lives here. I came to ask for his advice. He lives somewhere close by. I am not used to roaming around alone... my entire life...'

'Yes, yes, just six or seven houses ahead... I think he lives in 345,' Ma said.

'Yes, yes, that is the number. I was counting the numbers on the houses when you called out to me. God bless you! You feel such a sense of relief when you meet your own people in this city.'

'If you want, I can take you to Bhan sahib's house,' Ma offered a helping hand and Arundhati did not hesitate to accept it. 'Yes, it would be good if bahu came with me. Where should I ring the bell... where should I knock... I am very uncertain,' saying this Arundhati stood up.

Ma moved towards the gate saying, 'Come... come...' Arundhati embraced Kakni once more and followed Ma. 'I will take your leave. You must have your own work to do... and here I have been telling you my tale of woes.'

'*Arre,* what are you saying! A cow never feels the weight of its horns... you are our own. You must keep visiting us. Bring your husband along when he comes back.' As Kakni spoke, Arundhati made her way to the gate, adjusting her sari as she walked.

'Poor Arundhati, her life is full of troubles even today! May God have mercy!' With this comment, Kakni rested her head on the chair and closed her eyes. Sitting on the chair vacated by Arundhati, Shakti looked at Kakni. Sharda, who passed away fifty years ago, was still alive in Kakni's memory. Though we live on this earth, how much are we a part of it? Don't we really live in the world of memories? Our own world of memories and the universe of other people's reminiscences? We don't reside in just one place but in many. We live on in the memories of others often without our knowledge and even after we die and cease to exist on a physical plane. Then we no longer retain any relationship, not even with our own death!

Kakni was sitting with her eyes closed. What lies behind these closed lids and what has been lost forever? Shakti thought. It is so strange that the same Kakni who today reminisced about events that occurred over sixty years ago and who recognised an elderly woman who was young then, often forgets the names and faces of her own family. Just last evening she looked at her grandson's wife, Rashmi, without recognising her. After returning from office, Rashmi had picked up her cup of tea and come to sit near Kakni. Ma and Shakti were also in the same room. After a while Kakni gestured towards Ma who could not understand what her mother-in-law was trying to convey. Then Kakni tried to say something to Shakti. When Shakti went close to her in order to understand what she was saying, Kakni softly whispered in her ear, 'Doesn't this neighbour's daughter-in-law like being in her own house?'

'Which neighbour's daughter-in-law?' Shakti had asked in bewilderment. Kakni had gestured towards Rashmi and had spoken under her breath, '*Arre,* this one who has been sitting with her cup for so long... tell her to go home if she has finished her tea.'

Everyone had laughed at this incident and the atmosphere was full of banter. Shakti was, however, thinking about that soft walnut housed inside a man's skull which had blood coursing through it and within whose cells if there was even a hair's breadth of difference, a man's behaviour could change unrecognisably. Why is it that some people remember everything while some have a fragmented memory, and others remember only what they want to recollect. What is memory after all? A leaking bucket of water? A diary which can gather the past and the future together? A sponge which is soaking up everything for the future? A computer which is storing information? A camera which is recording everything? Or a maze in which everything ultimately gets lost.

Once we reach the end of our lives, do we gradually turn away from the world around us and go and live in our distant land of memory? Living with Ammu in Allahabad, Shakti often thought about this, or rather she was forced to think about it. Ammu bid goodbye to her seventy-fifth year last month on the eighth day of the new moon but sometimes she would suddenly start behaving like the ninety-year-old Kakni. Then she would turn her face away from the present around her and go to live in some distant past. That time wouldn't last too long, it hadn't become a constant feature as in Kakni's case. Ammu did come back.

Ammu – her husband Ramesh's mother Rajni Raina – whom she had left in Allahabad for a fortnight with her sister-in-law since she had to visit her parents. Shakti had spoken to Ammu for the first time the day before her wedding when they were going to have the *Phoolon-ka-gehena* ceremony. Ammu had sent innumerable strings of sweet smelling jasmine and *harsingaar* and

Shakti was instructed over the phone that she should remove any other jewellery that she was wearing. Then Ramesh's sister-in-law and his sisters dressed her up making jewellery out of those strings of flowers. Necklace, bangles, earrings, armlet, waist belt, an ornament for the forehead and anklets for her feet – all were made of flowers. Even her hair was perfumed with the smell of jasmine flowers. When she looked at herself in the mirror she felt she looked like Kalidas' 'Shakuntala'. She was delighted. Her family was seeing this flower ceremony for the first time. They had never seen it in Kashmir, or in the house of any Kashmiri before. This was a custom adopted by the Kashmiris who had left Srinagar hundreds of years ago and had settled in U.P.

After banishment from Srinagar, by the time Shakti's family settled in Jammu, she had already completed her schooling. She was sent to Delhi for further studies where she met Ramesh at a friend's house. Ramesh was a friend of her friend's elder brother. Later she bumped into him in the Delhi University Arts Faculty, then in the Law Faculty canteen and many other places. The frequency of their meetings kept increasing and finally they decided to tie themselves in an unbreakable bond. For Shakti's family, this decision was a lucky chance. Ma was always worried that Shakti, living so far from her family in Delhi, might decide to marry some non-Kashmiri. When Shakti, on the contrary, informed them that the name of the boy was Ramesh Raina they were amazed. Kashinath Kaul left for Allahabad immediately with his wife to discuss the marriage proposal with Bhushan Lal Raina, Ramesh's father. However, when he met the family he was as surprised as he was overjoyed as he found that they were Kashmiris only in name. Bhushan Lal's great-grandfather had left Srinagar and settled in Allahabad, and now even the traces of *Kashmiriyat* left in the family seemed alien. The language was not the same and neither were the eating habits, festivals and culture.

Who knows whether it is banishment or escape when with time even the traces of a culture are gradually erased! On his way home Kashinath thought that perhaps even his descendents would someday encounter their culture in the same way one meets a stranger from one's country on some lonely street or tourist spot in a foreign country. Someone with whom one has no relationship but who nevertheless arouses a sense of joy within, because he belongs to that faraway land which was once ours and to which we once belonged.

The members of Ramesh's family living far away from Kashmir in Allahabad are now called 'old Kashmiris' and we are still 'new Kashmiris'. Who knows how long we will be able to protect our language and culture and how long we will continue to be called 'new Kashmiris'! he thought. Kashinath's soul trembled. He suddenly felt as though his future generations had been orphaned. As though all the water in the rivers, ponds, springs and waterfalls of Kashmir had evaporated, turned into steam and disappeared.

Shakti's mother-in-law, her Ammu, belonged to the Katju family of Allahabad which had also uprooted itself from Srinagar many generations ago. Now it was a respected and well-to-do family of Allahabad. A long time back, Ammu's great-grandfather, grandfather and father had struggled hard in life, changing jobs and homes, and had gradually established the reputation of the family. It was her grandfather who had finally bought a huge mansion next to Anand Bhavan from a British officer and settled there. The mansion was named 'Vishranti Kunj' meaning grove of repose.

Ammu's father, Trilokinath Katju, was a contractor who constructed many of the prominent buildings in Allahabad.

He also owned some shops. However during the struggle for Independence, he gradually started distancing himself from home and became very quiet. Then one day, he burnt his cloth shop and, following Bapu's command, lit a bonfire of clothes and became a *Swaraji* – a freedom fighter. There was complete panic in Vishranti Kunj. Trilokinath's father was convinced that his son had lost his mental equilibrium. So, people were sent to look for him. When he returned in the evening, he was wearing a khadi kurta and a Gandhi cap. After spending the night at home, he left Allahabad the next day without informing anyone. He did send a word through someone later that he was well and that no attempt should be made to find him.

Ammu's father was last seen at the Allahabad railway station, wearing handcuffs and accompanied by the police. Perhaps they were waiting for a train. The news that the well-known contractor and freedom fighter Trilokinath who had made a bonfire of clothes was in handcuffs at the station, spread like wildfire through the city. Rajni was studying in eighth class at the time.

The station was crowded with people who were shouting slogans. Rajni glimpsed her father from far away as she clung to her brother Narendranath's arm. It was a strange sight which she could never forget. Instead of a well-creased and starched kurta, a half-sleeved, dirty check kurta hung loosely on his fragile body. Underneath he was wearing an equally depressing pyjama issued by the prison of indeterminate length, which was neither a pant nor a half-pant. His face glowed with the fervour of sacrifice but weakness and exhaustion were not too far away. Rajni felt a sense of pride that she was his daughter. Later, one day, someone brought the news that Bauji had passed away in Naini jail.

When Rajni was old enough for marriage the family chose Bhushan Lal, the lawyer son of the high court judge Mr Raina, to be her groom. Rajni had completed her B.A. by this time. Later she would proudly tell her grandsons and granddaughters, 'I have studied demand and supply in English, just like you.'

Mr Raina wanted an educated bride for his son, so Rajni's marriage was fixed to Bhushan Lal. In the meanwhile, due to Rajni's excellent academic record and the status of the elders in the family, she was offered the post of special magistrate of the Allahabad Sessions court. Rajni and her family were overjoyed but their joy was short-lived. The bridegroom's family raised the objection that it wasn't possible for their son to practice law in the same court where their daughter-in-law was a magistrate, even an honorary one! So Rajni turned her face away from the job. She became Ammu after her marriage and took over the running of the household.

This day, at the age of seventy-five, Ammu would sometimes behave as though whatever happened sixty years ago was actually happening in the present. Kakni's behaviour at the age of ninety was, therefore, quite understandable, especially because she had grown so weak physically. Ammu was not in the same situation then why was it that even her memory would sometimes abandon the present and go to live in the distant past. Why do some of the openings in the fountainhead of memory sometimes get blocked by the dust of the present?

Shakti remembered that cold January night in Allahabad. Ammu had loaded herself with a pile of woollens. She was sitting under a quilt warming her feet on a hot water bottle when she suddenly called out, 'Bahu, bring my fur coat when you visit Vishranti Kunj next time. I won't be able to go out in this cold without it. You will have to get it. I have hidden it in the black trunk lying on the right side in my mother's prayer room. My fur coat...made of white fur...white as snow and soft as a rabbit...' Then she added with a slight smile, 'Uncle had brought it for me from Srinagar. Santosh always fought with me over that coat, so I hid it in Ma's trunk.' Shakti was left staring at her, dumbfounded, because Vishranti Kunj had been sold ten or fifteen years ago. Ammu, however, was still wandering around in it. 'I also had a similar fur purse...Mrs Roberts brought it from London. One day I kept my scholarship money – sixteen rupees – in it and believe me, it got lost the same day...it was very pretty. I kept saying that the *dhobi* had come into the room...he must have hidden it in his towel and taken it away...his house should be searched, but no one listened to me.'

Why was it that whenever Ammu retreated into the past, into a world of illusion, she always went back to her childhood? Was the coat just a fur coat or did it symbolise all those soft and warm days of her youth which she remembered and wanted to wrap around herself? Perhaps proximity to the threshold of death pulls one towards life and life draws one towards childhood...towards a new beginning! When children are healthy their mothers inhabit the margins of their lives but whenever they are unwell they remember their mothers and look for the protection of their embrace, taking shelter there. Is the memory of childhood a similar refuge?

A few days later Ammu suddenly asked Ramesh, 'Son, did you visit Vishranti Kunj? The *kaith* trees...are they the same or have they withered away? Do you remember the trees near the cottage?' The cup of tea which had been on its way to Ramesh's mouth abruptly came to a halt.

What is this mind? The intellect which keeps a watch on the mind does not have foreknowledge of every celebration, every instruction of the world of the mind. The poor intellect is alone. It must be blinking at times. And the world of the mind? It is a complete forest. A forest of memories! Who knows what is hidden in this forest of memories? This forest has innumerable weeds which often give the illusion of being trees and bushes.

As the mind gets tired in old age, why do we forget the present? Why do the joys and sorrows of countless happenings, festivals, occasions gathered during the course of life, which are our real riches, gradually slip through the chinks in our fists. The joys which we experienced with an exhilarating tremor, the sorrows which we clung to and cried, why do their memories fade away during life itself? Even before our material existence in this world has ended. Why are bundles of affectionate relationships abandoned in some dusty corner? Why is it that despite being alive we are no longer aware of what we have lost? The bundles become insignificant and we fail to feel them anymore. So, is this life? The play of memory in a transitory fair? And if there is no memory, there is nothing?

Do we return to memories of the past when there is nothing left? Till there is strength in the body, the mind rides high on the swing of memory. It moves backward and forward constantly. In old age the body lacks the energy to make this constant shift. Perhaps the mind finds it difficult to return to the present from the past. And the world calls this an aberration of the mind.

Doesn't she live in the pleasant memories of the past as well? Shakti thought. Doesn't her childhood and youth spent in Srinagar reside permanently within the dark recesses of her mind? Doesn't she sometimes want to get lost like Arundhati's husband and return to the days of her childhood? To shake out the old clothes stored in trunks and then put them back in order again! For her, Kakni was a personification of history, a history which once lived in the Valley of Srinagar and this day lived in a confused mind full of muddled memories. Or in an illusion of the past. Who knows till when? This unfortunate history will soon be covered with the dust of time and no one will be able to remove this dust. This collective subconscious is so ill-fated that when, after centuries, someone digs into its soil, there would be no relics or remains as there were in Harrappa and Mohenjodaro. No skeletons, no bones, because exile and displacement would have devoured those remnants. She felt her life was like a half-demolished house whose roofs had deliberately been broken with hammer blows. A three-storeyed house with innumerable rooms and no roof, whose ruined walls contain rubble from its own broken roofs. Mountains of rubble.

'Everyone accomplishes the journey of life carrying bundles of their good deeds of the past, leaning on the staff of longevity and marching to the beat of joy and sorrow.' Perhaps this saying of Papa is ultimately correct, Shakti thought. So why were all the people, who were fated to carry the weight of deeds done in their past lives, to pass through the varied portals of history and who were also destined to bear the pain of banishment on their backs, born only in this state? Why again and again? Why here? Why?

Shakti felt the blood had rushed to her brain. Oh, where was her mind travelling! Now she would probably get a terrible headache. The shadow of fear constantly chased her and sometimes transformed itself into a sandy wilderness of sorrow. Many causes were suggested for its occurrence – the intense heat of summer, a gust of wind, an empty stomach or one too full. And doctors called it a 'migraine'. She knew that the real cause lay in her mind. The mind which once dislodged could never find its roots, which was always displaced. A displaced mind!

The rush of blood to her brain increased. Her eardrums reverberated faster and faster. As if blood wanted to spill out of her skull. In her bursting blood vessels she could feel the thudding of memories. She wished to get some comfort from putting an ice pack on her head. She wished the throbbing of these memories would congeal and freeze into ice. Or become like the lights used on festivals in which the entire string would switch off even if one of the tiny bulbs fused.

'Shakti, bring Kakni in. It is getting dark.' Shakti was startled to hear her mother calling out from the kitchen window. She had no idea when Ma came back or when the evening entered into the cloak of the night.

'Beta, wake Kakni up and bring her in…she has dozed off sitting in the chair…she must be tired. And go and fold your hands in front of the *thali* of fish and rice.' Then after a while she added, 'We have lost our home and our city but we don't have to abandon our customs and festivals. Today is the Saturday of the dark half of the lunar cycle in the month of *Paush*. Go and place some rice as offering for our *grehdevta*.' Ma had come out. Seeing Shakti in a state of uncertainty, she woke Kakni up, helped her to get up and took her inside.

When Shakti went into the kitchen she found a large *thali* of bell metal with two pieces of cooked fish, a small amount of rice and a piece of raw fish covered with vermilion which she had to leave on the roof for the *grehdevta* – the guardian deity of the home. The thought of *grehdevta* brought a sarcastic smile to her lips. *Grehdevta*! There was no ancestral home left, nor any land. She had always heard that every house had its own guardian deity. They had left their guardian behind when they were banished. Would he still be living in that ghostly empty house? she thought. Then he must be wandering around famished for so many years, in the narrow lanes and on the banks of the river. Or in the dark empty storage rooms which must be resonating with silence like the deep dark jungles of memory.

Unconsciously she started making small oval piles out of the rice just like the *pinds* offered to departed ancestors. Many *pinds*. Then she stopped and looked at them. Would she make these offerings, do *pinddaan*? Every breath she took in the memory of her beloved Kashmir was like a *pinddaan*, an offering to the past. So? Would she make the offering in the memory of the *grehdevta*? The *grehdevta* who was now the past, or a ghost. But what had she been doing up till now? Living in memory. Wasn't memory an offering to what had been lost?

Shakti picked up the *thali* with the oval piles of rice and slowly walked towards the stairs. Just as every house has a *grehdevta*, a resident deity, the body is also a home whose *grehdevta* is the soul, and the food of the soul, its fish-rice...what is it? she thought to herself. Perhaps... memory. But after being displaced, the memories fade away, generation after generation. Shakti looked at the piles of rice. Staring at them intently, she gradually climbed the stairs. Carefully and slowly. She was afraid that her memories would fall from the *thali* to the ground and be lost forever!

Reverse Whistle

'It has been three days already...not even one report has been typed. This blessed computer...this is the computer age but whenever you need it, it would just refuse to start! If the hardware is working fine, then there is a virus in the software...it just won't work...just sit and wait...oh! This bureaucratic system! When will the technician come...when will the computer be repaired...who knows! Huh! It isn't a virus, it's a headache!'

'...Virus.'

The nurse had started grumbling as soon as she put down the receiver. Hema, who was standing near the vacant stool, immediately guessed that the caller must have been some typist or computer expert who was expressing his inability to complete the report. In her irritation the nurse was pushing around the papers lying on the table which was placed against the wall of the tiny room. Hema thought it better to stay away from the ambit of her annoyance. But the nurse's last word 'virus' had lodged itself somewhere in her mind. She stepped out slowly.

Hema carried her body, weighed down by the burden of uncertainty and exhaustion, out of the emergency room. Now what? The nurse had given Veena jiji an injection at twelve o'clock, thanks to which she had finally gone to sleep. Three hours had elapsed since then. Hema had hoped that once the doctor finished his work in the OPD he would come her way and she would be able to talk to him. But she had been moving in and out of the room and in the verandah for the past three hours, waiting for him. She felt that he would arrive any moment. But many such moments passed by, full of hope and despair. Both together. Perhaps two facets of one idea. The split personality of human thought.

Standing outside the emergency, she had wanted to stop awhile and consider which way she should go but the word 'virus' had already rooted itself in her mind. This bristly word prevented any other thought from entering the doorway of her mind. So Hema's feet instinctively carried her towards the garden on her left. Perhaps searching for a place to sit. In the hope that they could rest if there was some place to sit down. It would be better if every part of the body could take care of its own comforts and responsibilities! One poor brain burdened by the weight of the entire body! And even the brain is not independent as the mind pulls its strings.

Hema's feet were moving ahead but the 'virus' was revolving in her mind. The software virus! Hardware and software, like the body and the mind. Then what would be the virus of the software?

Walking, she reached the old side of the hospital. A dilapidated, shabby building where mental patients were once locked up in rooms with iron grills in the windows. Now there were no patients but attendants to look after them could be found through agents. Things had changed. The hospital which was once bluntly called the 'mental asylum' was now known as the Hospital for Human Behaviour. A new building had also been erected for the patients, with windows and ventilators. Who knows if this new building will also make some place in Veena jiji's life for a window or a ventilator! Hema thought.

Hema felt a sense of suffocation inside the building despite so many windows and ventilators. Disturbed by this stuffiness, she roamed in the corridors and then came out into the open gardens. Why have such sprawling gardens been made here? When she looked at the building again, it seemed very small in comparison. Who knows how many half-fulfilled hopes are buried here! Mausoleums of helplessness! Can these spacious gardens situated against the backdrop of these mausoleums compensate for the loss of the throbbing vitality of life? The attempt to balance hopelessness and breathing lives! But isn't this just a futile attempt?

Hema, or rather her feet which wanted some rest, spotted a clean, empty parapet and moved towards it. As soon as she sat down Hema's gaze fell on a tree in front of her. Oh! This tree growing in the old part of the building must be around thirty-five or forty years old. A strong tree but the trunk was rough and cracked. The bark of the tree was dry, burnt and peeling off. The skin of a brown, burnt body. What unbearable anxiety could have caused the surface of the tree to become so blighted?

Stress is such a strange phenomenon! Why isn't there any barometer which can measure how, when and why people are affected by tension? Hema had recently read that during a study on stress the skin of rats, who were exposed to constant strong light and loud music for three or four days, became deformed.

In other words even an excess of life giving light and music can cause stress!

But what tensions would this tree have experienced? Perhaps it did not get adequate air because of the surrounding cement walls, or there may be a dearth of water or sunshine. That is why the bark is dry and anguished. The sap inside, the love inside, has dried up. Has the heart of this tree also become parched? Would that be surprising, Hema thought. Just as the mental state, the moods of individuals affect other members of a household they also impact the vegetation in the house. For years and years this tree must have felt the audible and silent cries of the patients cooped up like prisoners in this old building. How can anything flourish when there is misery all around!

Just then Hema heard the sound of a whistle coming from far away. Loud and deeply breathed whistles. One after another. Four or five times, perhaps. She had heard the same sound once or twice before as she strolled in the corridors waiting for the doctor. She had looked around to locate its source but she hadn't seen anybody. It seemed a little strange to hear the sound of the whistle as she looked at the mournful tree standing in the shadow of the dilapidated building. Who was calling whom? There was no one there except the ramshackle building, the cheerless tree, and her own dishevelled self. That was it. As a child if she saw anyone whistling she would be fascinated. She would also try to whistle but was always reprimanded, 'Girls from good families do not whistle.' In her youth, if she was tempted to turn and look at anyone who was whistling, the directives of Rajeev bhaiya and Veena jiji would act as an obstacle, 'Walk straight...let them whistle...how does it concern you?' She would not look back but somehow her heart would beat a little faster. That day, after so many years, at the age of thirty-five why did the sound of the whistle in that barren place made her feel so disturbed? Why?

Hema craned her neck and looked around to see who was whistling but there was no one there except the sound. She could see two children in school uniform walking at the spot where the road coming from the direction of the emergency snaked in between the OPD and the emergency, turned towards the left. So children were using this road through the hospital as a short cut even today! Hema saw herself, around twenty-five years ago, as a little girl wearing a blue skirt and white shirt walking down the same path. Her two tight plaits would be tied into loops with red ribbon flowers. Weighed down by her school bag. Excited at the thought of bypassing the long road and getting home early by using the shortcut. But at that time she was not aware that the shortcuts one takes in life are not always shortcuts. Sometimes one has to traverse them endlessly, just keep walking, moving down an unending road. Walking alone at times and sometimes with a solitary companion who has lost his way! We accompany this person not really thinking about whether he or she will reach any destination, or whether the place he or she reaches is the real destination. We just walk along by their side. On the other hand there are countless others who either drift along or lose their way, condemned to walk on an unknown path carrying the baggage of nagging thoughts on their backs or just lie abandoned, alone on pavements. Surrounded by a loneliness which sometimes gives a strange sense of desolation, at others, the terror of being trapped in a dark well, and at yet others the dread of being on an endless search for a safe haven in a land where kites and vultures hover over your head with their frightening wings outstretched.

Who had ever imagined that the young Hema, who walked down the road which cut between the OPD and the emergency on her way to and from school carrying the burden of her school bag, would one day walk the same road weighed down by the burden of her sister's sorrow. Years later, alone, with slow and weary steps.

Hema's raised neck drooped and she could actually feel the weight of a bundle on her back, one filled with pus. So much pus that if you tied a knot on one side it would ooze out from the other side. And if you tied another knot it would drip from a third edge. No medicine could help dry it up. Not even a couple of affectionate words. But she had nevertheless decided that she would lavish all the affection she possessed on her Veena jiji, even though every attempt seemed to be going down the drain.

Suddenly, as she touched her right arm, she felt that her skin had also started cracking like the bark of the tree in front of her. She touched her other arm. Then her cheeks, forehead and neck – all felt like the scabs of past wounds had accumulated instead of falling off. The more she tried to sneak into Veena jiji's world the more the scabs increased in number. Who knew what Veena jiji was carrying in the receptacle of her mind as she wandered through days and nights. Suddenly Hema stood up, agitated. She could see her own scabs but what about Veena jiji's? Reproaching herself she walked towards the shortcut. She could once again see, before her, the young Hema rushing to her way home. She would be in a hurry to get home since half-time in school. That morning Veena jiji had said that she would make the saffron *halwa* with raisins which Hema loved. When she reached home Veena jiji had first fed her the *halwa*. Hema was eating and Veena jiji was sitting in front of her, watching her with a smile.

'Jiji, have you had some?' Hema had asked her, stuffing a spoonful of *halwa* in her mouth.

'When I see you eating I feel like I have already eaten,' she answered with a smile. 'You silly girl, you eat like a famished man gorging on *kheer*.'

'Not *kheer*, Jiji, *halwa*. Made by you...yellow *halwa*.' And putting the bowl on the stool Hema had gone and put her arms around her jiji. Jiji kissed her hair and said, 'You are such a dear girl!'

'Why do you love me so much?' Veena jiji was lost in thought when Hema asked this question. Hema often asked this question and every time Veena jiji seemed to lose herself somewhere far away. This time Hema was determined, 'Tell me, Jiji...tell me...why do you love me so much?'

'So that you never feel that no one loves you.' Jiji tried to halt the questions.

'But why should I feel that? Everyone loves me...papa, Rajeev bhaiya, you...everyone.'

'Yes, but sometimes...'

'Sometimes? But why?'

'I don't know why! But at times I do feel it.'

'You feel that?' Hema asked and Veena jiji appeared to address the wall as she replied, 'When I was your age...yes, I was also in the third class, then one day...' Veena jiji abruptly stopped speaking.

'What happened that day?'

'Nothing.' Veena jiji tried to change the topic.

'What happened that day? Tell me, Jiji.'

'That day...that day I was getting ready for school,' Veena jiji had travelled to some far-off place. 'I saw ma's gold chain lying on the shelf. God knows why, I put the chain in my bag and left for school.'

'Then?'

'When I came back I found the house in turmoil because the gold chain had been lost. Everyone was wondering who could have taken it. No one had come to the house. The earth couldn't have swallowed it! Papa yelled at ma. He said she was becoming careless...hadn't taken care of it.'

'You still didn't tell anyone that it was with you?' asked Hema.

'No.'

'So?'

'Three days passed by. On the fourth evening papa asked me for a rubber and I put my hand into the bag to look for it. I rummaged around but I couldn't find it. He was standing there, waiting. I just couldn't locate the eraser. I turned my bag upside down so that I could find it and give it to papa.'

'And ma's chain?'

'It fell out of the bag. Ma was sitting close by on the floor, I think she was feeding Rajiv some *khichdi*. When she saw it she screamed, "My chain".'

'Then?'

'I was confused...I was sweating with fear. My cheeks...my cheeks...they became numb.' Hema could see the same fear in Veena jiji's eyes even that day, after so many years. Jiji was saying, 'Ma asked, "So you took the chain?" But I did not reply. How could I? I was shivering with fear.'

'And papa?'

'He asked me in a thundering voice, "Why did you take the chain?" '

'You still kept quiet?'

'No, I was totally at a loss for words. In my panic I blurted out the truth.'

'What?'

'That ma did not give me any *kheer* when I asked for it. Ma said, "*Arre*, I just made a little bit of *sago kheer* for Rajeev..."' Veena jiji suddenly became silent. Looking at her face even Hema could not question her any further. Veena jiji seemed to be turning into someone else. Then after a while she spoke again, almost as if she was speaking to herself, 'Papa again asked angrily why had I taken the chain. What was I going to do with it? I told the truth again...that...that I thought ma doesn't give me *kheer*, so I will hide her chain...she won't find it even if she looks for it.'

Hema was listening quietly as Veena jiji travelled backwards, 'Papa gave me a hard slap on my ear,' Veena jiji said, rubbing her ear. 'My head reeled and my ear started bleeding.'

'Oh! So since then you have had pain in your ear and sometimes pus also comes out of it?'

Veena jiji's thoughts scattered. She stood up dusting her clothes, picked up the empty bowl and spoon from the three-legged stool and walked towards the kitchen. Hema called out from behind, 'But, Jiji, why did you do it?'

Veena jiji returned to the present, 'Because I wanted ma to love me and I felt she only loved Rajeev.'

'And me?'

'You? You were not even there,' Hema started laughing and there was a faint smile on jiji's face. Hema got up and went to Veena jiji in the kitchen. 'Didn't ma love you?'

'She did...but I am silly, aren't I?' said Veena jiji as she gently tugged at Hema's plaits, 'You don't need to think about all this. You have me, don't you...to love you a lot.'

'To my heart's content?'

'Yes, yes, to your heart's content!'

'Why not even more?'

At this statement Hema's innocent grin collided playfully with Veena jiji's wise but hesitant smile.

Veena jiji was Hema's elder sister and the eldest child of the family. Hema knew since childhood that Veena jiji was the only child of her father Nand Kumar's first wife. Perhaps this was why she did not address Hema's maternal uncle Manohar mama as 'mama'. Veena jiji had another mama who would bring clothes only for her whenever he visited. He would talk only to Veena jiji and then leave. After he left, Hema would ask Veena jiji what mamaji had brought for her and Veena jiji would say all the clothes were really for Hema. She could wear them when she grew older. But where did Hema have the patience! She would immediately put her tiny feet and hands into the oversized clothes and walk around trailing them all over the house. She wouldn't bother even if papa shouted at her. And then Veena jiji was always there to defend her. When Hema would finally get tired she would throw off the clothes, 'Now you wear them, Jiji.'

During his youth, Nand Kumar had come in search of a good job from Alwar to his friend in Delhi. This friend was a proofreader in a reputed newspaper. He got his friend Nand Kumar a job as a proofreader on daily wages for a few months. Nand Kumar was lucky enough to get a permanent job in the same office after some time. His friend lived outside the city in a neglected suburb. There was no residential area close by. Just a hospital for mental patients, so one would encounter some rickshaw-pullers and tonga drivers, sometimes even a car. Nand Kumar rented a room in the same colony and made Delhi his home. His office was quite far away but the place was pocket-friendly. Then he also had a dream inspired by his friend's example. A dream which was like a helpless cry in the world of power, that he could buy a small piece of land in the colony and manage a roof over his head.

In the meanwhile, the news that Nand Kumar had got a permanent job reached Alwar like a bolt of lightning. His mother immediately fixed a match for him. When Nand Kumar arrived in Alwar with a few gifts bought from his salary, he was married off at an auspicious time. Who knows whether the time was really auspicious because when their first child Veena was six months old Nand Kumar's wife died of a tumour in the stomach. Her grandmother immediately arrived from Alwar and took charge of little Veena. But how long could this have gone on? So worldly-wise relatives started looking for matches for Nand Kumar from the thirteenth day of his wife's death.While one relative lamented about the difficulties in caring for a six-month-old infant while doing a full-time job, another referred to the difficulties of running a household.

Nand Kumar's father also suffered this massive problem because he could not leave his wife in Delhi for too long. Then if his daughter-in-law had left a grandson he could have suggested taking the child to Alwar. Looking after a granddaughter was too much of a responsibility. All these thoughts had already begun to churn in his mind soon after his daughter-in-law's death. So, he fixed Nand Kumar's marriage with the sister-in-law of a distant relative among the many who had gathered. After the thirteenth day, Nand Kumar and everyone else travelled to Alwar and there he was married off in a simple, homely ceremony to Lakshmi Devi.

Lakshmi Devi belonged to a family of Kota stone merchants. She had barely started dreaming about life in Delhi when she was transported to a box-like home in a far-flung suburb of the city. Poverty resonated there like the rattling of a pebble in an empty box. And then the sisters and brothers-in-law who escorted her to Delhi placed the six-month-old Veena in her lap as soon as they entered the house and then disappeared.

Lakshmi Devi was a good-natured woman. In such circumstances she banished her dreams to a corner and took on the responsibilities of looking after the household and a six-month-old child. When her son was born after two-and-a-half years she became so engrossed in him that Veena was pushed into a far corner. Perhaps the same corner in which Lakshmi Devi had pushed her own dreams. The dreams had gradually faded away, so perhaps Veena fitted into the same space. In any case Veena was a girl and not even her own; she was the child of her husband's first wife. So she gradually faded to the edges of Lakshmi Devi's consciousness. But Veena was like the small change which lies forgotten in some corner of the pocket and come in useful at odd times. She proved to be a great help in many important and insignificant ways in her brother Rajeev's life.

Rajeev's birth, in a sense, orphaned Veena. When she saw her parents lavishing their affection on her brother she felt there must be something lacking in her. Then she would scrutinise Rajeev carefully. She found that she really was wanting in some ways. Bhaiya's body and limbs were quite different from hers. Perhaps that was why she did not get any affection after his birth. The entire household revolved around Rajeev and his activities. Every chuckle of the infant was remarked upon again and again and Veena would hear all this quietly sitting in her corner. Gradually she almost stopped speaking to her parents. She spoke or fought with them only in her mind.

Veena had started going to school. She also helped around the house and with her brother. After some time she noticed that her mother's belly was swelling once again. Ma was pregnant. Hema was born around five years after Rajeev. Veena always felt Hema was like her. Both from the point of view of physicality and the attitude of their parents towards them. The routine of the household did not revolve around Hema after she was born. Rajeev bhaiya was still the lynchpin of the house. Now it was his mischievous deeds rather than his smiles which were remarked upon.

Veena would now come back from school quite happily. The joy of feeling her finger clutched tightly in little Hema's fist would draw her home. When the little fist refused to let go of her finger the innocent Veena would feel as though she had regained all the affection in the world of which she had been bereft earlier. At least there was someone who wanted her company. Who wouldn't leave her. If anyone in the world loved her, it was Hema, with her little feet and hands.

At the time of Hema's naming ceremony Manohar mama arrived from Kota and stayed on in his sister's house. He helped his sister with the household marketing and also carried on his discussions with contractors regarding his business.

Around this time, one day, Veena's mother asked her to heat milk for Rajeev bhaiya. As she started walking out of the kitchen with the glass of hot milk her foot hit a shallow metal basin, and she couldn't balance the glass of milk. The milk spilled on her frock and her stomach was badly burnt. Ma yelled from inside, 'It was such a small thing…you couldn't even manage that! How many things can I take care of! How many people can I look after!'

Manohar mama helped his sister out by applying balm on Veena's stomach. After this incident, every morning and evening Manohar mama would very diligently make Veena lie down, raise her frock, and apply the balm slowly. To avoid disturbing his sister and her children he would take Veena into another room at such times. One day his hand wandered above and below her abdomen as he applied the balm. Veena caught his hand and said, 'Not here.'

'Keep lying down…keep lying down,' Mama said, as his hands continued to roam. Veena tried to get up but he held her down by placing his heavy leg over hers. In the evening when he called Veena to apply the balm she did not answer, nor did she come out. He called out once again. Ma got very angry and shouted at Veena to go and put the balm. Sitting on her string bed she yelled, 'Why don't you listen? Have you become deaf? The poor man is calling you and you are refusing to even respond. What is wrong with you? Go to his room immediately.' Veena continued to sit next to Hema though she was shivering with fear. Ma lost her temper and got up and dragged Veena towards Manohar's room, 'Go, get the balm applied, you stubborn girl.'

Veena timidly tried to say something, 'I don't want to put any balm…'

Ma just pushed her towards Manohar, 'Quiet! Don't you dare utter a single word…' Then she told Manohar, 'Please apply it, brother. If by some mischance it gets infected, I am the one who will have to look after her.'

The next moment Veena, with a tear-stained face and wiping her nose, lay down on the string bed and Manohar mama pulled up her frock and even pushed down her underwear in order to put the salve properly.

Veena's younger sister Hema was not even two years old when ma suffered from a bout of jaundice. Once ten-year-old Veena took on the responsibilities of the house and the kitchen during the mother's illness, she was permanently saddled with these chores. Ma's jaundice worsened and she finally passed away leaving the little desolate Hema in Veena's lap.

Manohar mama came again once during the obsequies of his sister. He suggested that he should take Veena and Rajeev to Kota for a few days in order to give Nand Kumar some breathing space. Oozing insincere affection he added, 'They will feel better there in the company of the other children of their age group.' Though Nand Kumar remained silent he mentally gave his acceptance. He thought the children would be glad of the diversion. Their dadi had already arrived from Alwar to take charge of Hema and the kitchen. Veena trembled with fear when she heard about going to Kota; she felt like her entire body was slathered with salve. She gathered her courage and told her grandmother, 'Dadi, I will stay near Hema... with you.' Dadi felt it was a good idea as it was very difficult to take care of a two-year-old child in an unfamiliar ambience and do all the household work all alone at her age. Mama had to swallow his chagrin and leave with only Rajeev.

Everyone in the house had come to accept that Veena was a girl of few words. She would become nervous at the smallest of things. She only chatted and looked happy when she was with little Hema. Shouldering the responsibility of looking after her brother and sister and helping dadi in her work gradually distanced Veena from her studies. She had also become slow in completing any work, however small. If she did one thing, another job would be neglected and the third forgotten. Somehow she reached the eighth class but she couldn't clear her examinations. She got a compartment in two subjects. Despite diligent efforts she could not pass and gradually lost interest in her school and school bag. She would get so busy with housework that she would end up missing school. Finally, dadi told Nand Kumar that if Veena had no interest in school and couldn't cope with it there was no point in sending her to school! She should look after the house. And this was exactly what happened.

Dadi was also relieved and she returned to Alwar for a few days. Then Hema's mausi suggested that she should send one of her daughters for a few days to help Rajeev and Hema. She had, after all, been blessed with six daughters, so she sent her eighteen-year-old and eldest girl Krishna to Nand Kumar mausa's place during her vacations.

The atmosphere in the house changed with Krishna's arrival. Nand Kumar also started spending more time at home. Card games were played. A carrom board was bought by her uncle at Krishna's request. She was now the pink queen of carrom in the house and Nand Kumar was the expert whose fingers danced up and down on the carrom board. Veena had never seen her father so happy.

That day radish *paranthas* had been cooked in the house. Rajeev and Hema had eaten while Veena was still sitting and eating her food. When Krishna brought the last *parantha* for her uncle, he slowly caressed her thrice from shoulder to waist as he was praising her. Then he took a piece of his *parantha* and put it in Krishna's mouth.

'Mausaji, what are you doing…the stove is burning in the kitchen,' Krishna said with a laugh. Nand Kumar pressed her thigh, forcing her to keep sitting, 'Sit down…eat…Veena will switch off the stove.' As soon as Veena heard her name she left her half-eaten *parantha* and walked towards the kitchen. But on the way she felt as though someone was putting salve on her prone body and gradually the salve-coated hand was reaching for her underwear. Her body tingled as she reached the kitchen and heard the laughing voices of Krishna and her father in the background. She sat on the low wooden stool in front of the stove. Suddenly she was filled with a sense of revulsion. One part of her wanted to vomit, the other part told her to tear off her own skin and throw it into the garbage. Papa and Krishna's playful words were mingling with the noise of the stove.

The fifteen-year-old Veena had become even more lonely in a house full of people. She wanted to be detached from her body just as she was cut off from the other members of the household. She wanted her mind to be totally disconnected from her body. Why did papa's voice sound exactly like Manohar mama's? She was convinced that her papa would even have started looking like Manohar mama. What are these relationships? Who is a 'mausa'? Who is a 'mama'? Who is a 'father'? Why do they all look alike? Her heart started beating faster and she felt like a nail had been pushed into her head. She was perspiring. Her tongue was trapped between her teeth. She felt giddy and fell in front of the stove stiffening into unconsciousness.

Now she only used to worry about Hema's whereabouts. Why hasn't she returned from school yet? Why is there a delay of even five minutes? She has gone to visit the neighbours, has she decided to adopt them now? Is she laughing and chatting with her friend's brother?

Her friend's uncle is visiting...is Hema playing cards with him?

'*Arre*, why did you stay so long at Anita's?'

'We were playing cards.'

'Cards! Are you a grandmother that you sit and play with your elders?'

'But there were no elders there, Jiji...'

'I know everything! I am sure her uncle must have come from Bareilly...you must have been playing cards with him.'

'No, Jiji...'

'You think I am stupid? There is no need to go to anyone's house. You will leave home only to go to school and then you will come straight back home...'

Veena jiji's love and indulgence would blanket these minor scoldings and restrictions.

As she grew up Veena's behaviour began to change. With a mind like a closed fist her body was gradually slowing down. She was taking more time to do everything. If she was washing rice at the tap, she would keep on washing it for long. If she was sweeping the room, the broom would refuse to leave her hand. And then there were the unpredictable fits. Now Nand Kumar finally got worried. If people heard about Veena's behaviour and fits it would be difficult to find a match for her, he thought. So he married off the nineteen-year-old girl to the son of a foreman in his own office. The boy was a clerk in a government school.

In a house full of brothers and sisters-in-law Veena's slowness was dismissed as the shyness of the new bride for a month or so. But after a while everyone noticed that when the new bride sat down to clean the dal she would go on cleaning it endlessly. Neither Veena nor anyone else realised that while she sat with the platter of dal, misfortune slowly tiptoed in and threw away all the pebbles of happiness from her life. Veena bore the scoldings and taunts of her in-laws for a year-and-a-half. Then one day her father and mother-in-law summoned Nand Kumar and told him to take her away. Veena's mother-in-law folded her hands and sarcastically remarked, 'Bhaisahib, enough! Please take this sacred offering away.' Nand Kumar tried to argue and explain but finally Veena went back home.

At that time Hema was still in school but the changing environment at home forced her to mature quickly. Rajeev somehow managed to complete his B.A. and started working in Rohtak. For a few years he came home regularly every weekend but gradually these weekends became sporadic. He even married his friend's sister and settled permanently in Rohtak. In any case, what was there to draw him home except the responsibilities of an old father, a mentally-challenged and abandoned sister and another one of marriageable age!

Relatives and neighbours would often tell Hema to get some medical treatment for Veena. Whenever she mentioned this to papa she got a standard answer, 'It is easy to talk…I have neither the time nor the money…*arre,* she has always been like this…she is not mad. Does she ever try to hurt anyone? She is a bundle of idleness; just doesn't move her limbs fast enough. Why do you pay attention to all this useless talk…concentrate on your studies.'

Hema would once again suggest softly that the hospital was so close by and they could perhaps visit it once. At this papa would get irritated and say, '*Arre,* that is a hospital for mad people…they keep the patients in chains, torment them with injections and electric shocks…will you be able to bear the sight of your sister screaming and suffering?' And Hema would be left in a dilemma.

She also felt that perhaps Veena's very nature was like that. She would only get worried when Veena would suffer from the occasional fits. But her grandmother had told her that there was no cure for such attacks. At such times Veena jiji would be made to smell a leather shoe and she would recover in a few minutes. As far as her behaviour was concerned, dadi said she had always been timid and a loner since her childhood. She did not enjoy company. She was even reluctant to address her mama as 'mama' and papa as 'papa'. She was so busy thinking the whole day that even her limbs had become inert.

When Hema went to college she learnt through her study of Psychology – a subject she took because her friend had opted for it – that the mind can also become ill just like the body. Though the mind is not physically visible, yet it can be understood through the actions and behaviour of a human being. The mind has no separate entity; rather every individual identity is, knowingly or unknowingly, dependent upon the mind.

This subject interested Hema so much that she borrowed library books on psychology which were beyond the scope of her syllabus and discussed it for hours with her teacher.

Gradually her interest took her so far that after her B.A. she chose Child Psychology as a subject in her B. Ed. Later, as a teacher in a small government school, she peeped into the tiny minds of the children. If she saw any dark and shadowy experiences etched there she got immense satisfaction in replacing them with the rainbow colours of the child's own imagination.

In fact, the human psyche was of such interest to her that even this day, as she waited on this road between the emergency and the OPD for the doctor, she could only pass her time with reflections on the 'mind' or the 'subconscious'. Doctors say the mind *controls* human behaviour, it rules the brain. In other words our body is controlled by the mind. First, an idea enters the mind, then it is contemplated, and then accordingly the brain goes into action. The proper balance or relationship between ideas, thought-process and implementation keeps the mind healthy and whenever there is an imbalance between these three the mind becomes unwell. Just like the traffic lights on the road – red, yellow and green. If they are properly synchronised the flow of traffic remains smooth and if there is any dissonance between the three, the game is messed up . There are accidents, or traffic jams!

The thought of the word 'game' brought a thin, painful smile to Hema's face. Life is a game which is not in our control; it is in the hands of the mind. What is this mind like? How large? How small? How long? How broad? Even psychologists have not been able to glimpse it yet!

Dadi used to say that Lord Krishna revealed his essential nature to Arjun in the *Bhagwad Geeta*. Using examples from the cosmos, he had compared himself to the moon among the planets. And the Sanskrit teacher used to call the moon 'the mind' because the moon was born from the mind of God. Then why does the controller of the body or the Almighty, which is the mind, behave so oddly at times? Different from others! Sometimes the mind makes its own separate frail shelter despite living within the bounds of home. What would the basement of this shelter be like? Haunted, perhaps!

Veena jiji had gradually shrunk within the walls of her ghostly refuge. Even far away from Hema, very far. If Hema tried to peep into Veena's secret world she felt a sense of fear bubbling inside her own self; like someone looking down from a great height. She could feel the waves of thought in her mind rising and receding.

Why does this only happen to some of us? Hema was thinking. Why do we start inhabiting different worlds? The conscious and the subconscious world, like shadow and light. Sometimes we – the inhabitants of the world of light – wander into the world of shadows but the residents of the shadowy world are its permanent residents who can never return. Not even if they want to. Gradually the doors of the world of light are so tightly shut for them that they are forced to wander about the roads and streets with their subterranean minds. Or they are placed in some small building like this one placed incongruously amidst wide open spaces and gardens. Here they are given treatment to shore them up the weakened or broken walls between the worlds of light and shade. Perhaps the medicines make them numb to most feelings! This may be the reason why Veena jiji sometimes gets up in the middle of a winter night and starts bathing with cold water, Hema thought.

When clouds gathered in the sky and darkened the day to evening, Hema was startled and looked at her watch. It was five o'clock. Who knows, the doctor might have come! She walked towards the emergency.

She had just walked ahead a little when she heard the sound of the whistle once again. The closer she came to the emergency, the louder the sound grew. Then she noticed that a woman, standing with a hand on her waist near the door of the nurse's room and looking out, was the one who was whistling. Hema's gaze was fixed on her. She had a sleek body and was wearing a well-fitting black top and a red below-the-knees polka-dotted skirt. Short, almost boy-cut hair. The confidence of prosperity on her face. A rather subdued looking policeman, standing some steps away, was probably escorting her.

Hema's eyes met those of the woman when she came near the door. The whistling abruptly came to a stop. The woman standing in the middle of the doorway continued to stare at Hema. Hema realised that she must be a patient. She asked her politely, 'May I enter?'

'Call me madam,' the woman replied sternly while continuing to stand in the doorway.

Hema's eyes were suddenly filled with gentleness and in an even softer voice she asked, 'Madam, may I go in?'

Now the lady took her hand off her waist and moved aside so that Hema could enter the room. The woman turned to look into the room. Hema had reached Veena jiji's bed by then. From behind her she heard, 'By the way, you can call me Sangeeta.' And having said this, she went out.

Sangeeta! Who could she be? Why is she here? There is a policeman with her. She must be involved in some case, Hema thought. Whenever she came to the hospital with Veena jiji she encountered all kind of strange people. And this woman had bestowed herself with the honorific 'madam'. There were many patients there who mistook themselves for what they were not. Last time a patient had stopped her and asked, 'You are Hema Malini, aren't you? I saw you in *Seeta and Geeta*.' Hema was bewildered.

Suddenly Hema remembered the Sardarji. Once before, when she had come here, she had heard a voice as she walked in the verandah outside the emergency. Someone was walking behind her saying, 'Madhouse, hospital... they have brought me here... lunatics! They have forgotten that this must have been built by the whore who ruined me. And that old man? Love... love, the love of children. All rubbish... no one ever loved me... just one...only one...P-85...but...not even him any longer.' The voice died away for a while. Hema was shaken. Turning back she had seen an elderly sardar who was walking along, talking to himself. Hema tried to recall his face but she couldn't, perhaps because despite turning back to look at him, her eyes hadn't managed to capture his face. Because not just her eyes but her entire body had been concentrating on hearing his babble.

Veena jiji was still sleeping and the doctor had not yet arrived. Even the nurse was not around. This was the nurse's room and a bed had been put in it only out of necessity. There were two beds in each of the other rooms. Hema came out and her curiosity made her eyes search for Sangeeta in the other rooms. She looked into one room and saw a young man on the bed with an old lady sitting next to him on a stool, half-asleep. The old woman became alert as soon as she saw Hema, 'Are you looking for the doctor, daughter? It is evening and he still hasn't come. Sitting idle such terrible thoughts come to mind that one is terrified.'

With a polite smile Hema said, 'He must be on his way.' The old lady got up and came out of the room. Standing in the verandah, she asked Hema, 'Which room are you in?'

'The nurse's room.'

'What is your relationship with the patient?'

'My sister.'

'Elder?'

'Yes, older.'

'What happened?'

'Nothing, she is just very quiet...depressed.'

'Don't tell me...this depression has ruined my house.' Adjusting the edge of the sari on her head, the old lady said, 'He is my son. He was like a mine of diamonds...but destiny! This sorrow is going to destroy me. God gave me a child in my old age. I wish he had also given him health. But no, he is punishing me for the sins of my past lives.'

'What happened to him?'

'If anything had happened I would have been able to understand but what can I say, daughter, I can't understand anything. I sent him off to study happily, but he was back in two months.'

'He left his studies?'

'Not just his studies, he abandoned life itself. We tried all kinds of medicines, did whatever anyone suggested. *Sarpgandha, Ashwagandha, Brahmi*... tried everything but it made no difference... everything remained just the same.'

'What had happened?'

'Who knows? If he told us anything clearly, at least we would have known.What is it called... that ragging... where they trouble boys . . .that is all he keeps repeating. He says they wouldn't let him sleep on the bed and the older boys would keep them awake all night and beat them with pillows... he doesn't say anything beyond this... he just ran away from the hostel. Now he alone knows the truth. His father tried very hard to persuade him to go back but he wouldn't. He would just sit by himself in his room. Once...' The old woman stopped speaking. Hema waited silently. Then the woman spoke again slowly as though she was swallowing water, 'Once he even drank something. God knows from where he got something like poison... there was so much froth coming out of his mouth. We took him to the hospital. His stomach had to be washed out to save him. But the problem remained as it is... and we also had to deal with the police and the law.'

'Is this the first time you have brought him here?'

'No, we had shown him in the OPD earlier. But now he becomes violent very quickly. Yesterday his sister said something and he threw a cup of tea at her so hard that it broke her nail. It had to be taken off. She just had to bear the pain.'

Hema could only say, 'Oh!'

'A few days ago he saw his sister on the street and slapped her. She has no occasion to talk to men but he can't even bear her talking to girls. Now tell me if girls don't talk to each other who will they talk to, animals?'

Just then they saw the doctor walking along with Sangeeta and the nurse following them. A few steps behind all of them, was the policeman. When the old lady saw them she said, 'Thank God the doctor has come…I better get back to my room,' and walked towards her room.

Hema stood against the wall and the group passed her and reached Sangeeta's room. Hema also walked to the room and stood outside with the policeman. The doctor checked Sangeeta's blood pressure. Then he said, 'It is your third day here. Till yesterday it was OK, why is your pressure so high today?'

'I had sex last night,' Sangeeta answered in a calm voice. The doctor was nonplussed and kept checking her pulse. Hema came back to Veena jiji's room. She wondered, could Sangeeta's statement be true? No. How is it possible? She has been here for three days…in the hospital with the policeman standing outside. So? It must be her imagination.

Just then the doctor entered the nurse's room. He checked Veena's pulse, 'Listen, we have to shift her to the ward. Would you like a private…?'

'No, Doctor sahib, shift her to the general ward,' Hema replied before he could complete the sentence.

'Fine. We will shift her in the morning. But first we will have to take her to the general hospital for some tests. We feel there is a protein deficiency…lungs will also have to be X-rayed, only then can we begin her treatment. Till then she will be under observation.'

'Doctor sahib, she is very weak.'

'She would be, she is very anaemic. Let's see…she may require a blood transfusion.'

The doctor, nurse and Hema looked at the door where Sangeeta was standing saying, 'Yes, she is anaemic…she needs blood…treat her well…don't worry…I will pay for it, I have lots of money.' Then she went off nonchalantly.

When Hema came out after the doctor left she saw Sangeeta sitting on a ledge whistling every two minutes. The policeman was standing a few steps away smoking in a bored manner. When Hema looked more carefully she saw that the woman did not breathe out as she whistled, instead she sucked the air inwards. So, she was actually whistling backwards. Hema was quite surprised. She felt like talking to Sangeeta. She came close to her slowly and said, 'Please teach me how to whistle.'

Without turning her neck to look at her Sangeeta answered very solemnly, 'You won't be able to learn,' and started whistling again. The backwards whistle.

At night Hema heard some voices. One of them was Sangeeta's and she seemed to be insisting on sleeping outside her room in the fresh air while the nurse tried to argue with her against it. Sangeeta was saying that she did not want to sleep in a grave. The nurse could not give her permission to sleep outside because of the rules of the hospital. When Hema came out in the morning she saw Sangeeta sleeping in the corridor on sheets of newspaper with the uniformed policeman leaning against the wall and dozing nearby.

Hema had heard the whistle intermittently throughout the night. Sangeeta must have gone to sleep at dawn. Just then she saw another policeman approaching with a foreign girl. The girl was African, perhaps Nigerian. A dessicated, thin body. Teeth shining white in her face. A short grimy shirt worn over baggy jeans. A bottle of mineral water in her hand.

The new policeman waved his hand in a salute to the one sitting in the verandah who opened his eyes and said, 'Come along, brother…you also do your duty.'

The new policeman took the girl straight to the nurse's room. Hema shifted from the door to make place and came and sat on the stool kept near Veena jiji's bed. The policeman went out after handing the young lady over to the nurse. The nurse made the girl sit on a chair and spoke to her in a friendly tone, 'So how are you now?'

'I am sad…don't even feel like bathing.' The girl answered and then opened the cap of the bottle and started dinking. Hema looked carefully at the girl. She was right. She evidently hadn't bathed for weeks.

The new policeman was asking the other in the verandah, 'When did you come here?'

'Three or four days ago. One has to look after the wretch night and day!'

The new policeman spoke in a slightly hushed tone, 'Why are you complaining…yours is like white bread…look at what I had to escort here from Tihar jail.'

'You are never going to change, *saala*…' the policeman in the verandah said smiling.

'Why is she lying here with her legs spread out like this, didn't she get a room?'

'Madam can't stay in the room! She has got into the habit of roaming around. Wants to stay out in the open. We even caught her in the park. She was whistling away lying on a bench. But she kicks anyone who comes near her. Horsy bitch!'

The new policeman stifled his laughter and spoke in a low mumble, 'When a mad mare kicks, she kicks really hard but this one is quite something. She evidently didn't let you come near her.'

The policeman in the verandah was a little embarrassed. Then he stood up dusting his trousers, 'No one even from home comes to pick up the wretch! In any case no one stops her when she wanders around the streets. She should be kept locked up. Two or three manly slaps will take away all her fizz. I've heard her husband is dead, she has two children, in-laws and parents. It has been three days now and no one has even peeped in . . . if no one comes today God knows where they will throw her . . . anyway, it will be good riddance for me.'

The new policeman said, 'Mine is no less. She looks like a needle, as though she was barely alive. But she was caught selling drugs . . . God knows why these women leave their countries and come here to study!'

Hema's stool was next to the window which was ajar. She heard an almost indistinct whisper, 'Look how she is wriggling!' Sangeeta must have turned over, Hema thought. There was silence outside for a few minutes. Then she heard the voice of the new policeman, 'You are here, aren't you? I will just go to the bathroom for a minute. Keep an eye . . . don't let mine run away.'

'Yes, yes, go. Why just a minute, take your own sweet time,' the other policeman laughed.

Veena jiji was going to be shifted to the general ward. It was eleven o'clock. Hema was waiting for the doctor's written instructions. God knows why she suddenly remembered the old lady in the room opposite. Would she have eaten anything? Hema thought she would tell the old lady to go and eat something outside. She would sit with the lady's son in the meanwhile because Veena jiji was in a deep sleep under the effect of the injections.

When she came out she heard some commotion in Sangeeta's room. Perhaps someone had come to pick her up. The old lady was also standing in the verandah peeping into Sangeeta's room. When she saw Hema, she said softly, 'It is her brother...he has come to take her.'

A few minutes later a relieved-looking policeman, with a smile on his face, crossed the verandah on his way out. Behind him came a silent Sangeeta accompanied by a man.

Just then a long car halted at the gate. The driver opened the door. The man gestured politely to Sangeeta to enter first. He closed the door and and got in from the opposite door. Hema noticed Sangeeta was looking towards the emergency as though she was staring at a void. In that void she drew in a breath and started whistling. The same reverse whistle.

Evidently Sangeeta was not very concerned about the fact that she was going home, or that someone had come to fetch her. God knows since when she has had this habit of whistling backwards! Hema thought. Isn't this reverse whistle a part of her personality, a part which others may find odd and meaningless but which only reinforces her alienation from others? Why does she whistle in this strange manner and who does she whistle for! Does she whistle for someone, or is her whistle just a cry of pain emerging from her solitude?

The car started. Sangeeta was still whistling as she sat in the car. Like a solitary engine rushing backwards instead of forwards, drawing all the smoke into its own lungs. It couldn't move ahead, and who wants to accompany those who move backwards! There is no carriage attached to it, probably because the hook on the buffer is broken.

Hema's mind was in turmoil. God knows how many such people there must be in the world across cast, gender, social strata or the borders of countries, who are burdened by the grime of the past! Individuals driven by the fear of society, disappointment, terrorised into the suffocating dark corners of the mind! Are these people alive, or are they continuously dying! The termites of the mind gradually begin to erode the structure of the body. Why aren't the rules of nature the same everywhere? When leaves of the mind dry up and fall to the ground, why don't they become the manure for the growth of new leaves, buds and flowers?

How many such people do we throw out of our homes because they are like obsolete coins, which are of no value in the market or in our pockets? Often we deliberately try to leave them behind, or forget them somewhere by giving wrong addresses in hospitals, or by detaching our hands from theirs in crowded places.

The number of these people, who are like the thin edge of a river, is increasing in the world. Is the river broadening to swallow up the ocean? Intoxicated with the movement and the exhilaration of its waves the busy ocean does not realise that it is gradually drying up! Gradually, but constantly.

Sangeeta's car took the road leading towards the OPD as it moved to the main gate of the hospital. Hema suddenly felt as if Sangeeta, Veena jiji, the old lady's son and many others were whistling backwards. These reverse whistles were increasing day by day. Then her thoughts came to an abrupt halt as it struck her that perhaps for all those people *we* were whistling in reverse. Breathing out!

Paper Bastion

When the binding of a book falls apart, not only does its stitching unravel but its pages also get mixed up and lose their sequence. The book becomes just a disorganised bundle. That day Gopa had once again gone to the fort of Golconda, eleven kilometers away from Hyderabad, carrying the burden of her similarly disordered life. In front of her was the 'Victory gate' – the main entrance to the fort. The gate was named by Aurangzeb after he had conquered the fort. But it must have had another name before, Gopa thought. Like a woman whose identity changes after marriage and she comes to be known only by her 'master's' name…no one refers to her by that earlier name. Touching the stone wall, which had been constructed to conceal the 'Victory gate', Gopa murmured to herself, 'Purdah'. That was the name of this wall, which was made keeping the height and width of the 'Victory gate' in consideration. It was just large enough to conceal the gate from the view of the enemy. A curtain of stone!

Whenever Gopa entered the fort a host of stories and narratives accompanied her like the guides standing, waiting, at that gate of victory. That day she ignored the guides and moved forward briskly. A little ahead, she turned to the right after crossing the portico and the Bala Hissar gate. When there was no order left in her life why should she bother to view the fort in the proper sequence? She was familiar with each and every stone in it. As she was trying to decide which way to go, she saw a group of VIPs ahead with a guide who was explaining something to them. She moved forward till she was just at a little distance from the group and moved along with them.

'The fort is girdled by granite walls on three sides. The external wall is seventeen to thirty-four feet thick and it has eighty-seven semicircular bastions set into it which are fifty to sixty feet high. Four of these bastions are famous. I will show you three of them but we can only talk about the fourth.'

'Why?' one of the men in the group asked smiling.

'Because it no longer exists. Yes, sahib! This happened during the time when Abul Hassan Tana Shah was the sultan. He was a real thorn in the flesh of Aurangzeb who could not conquer this fort despite laying siege to it for eight long months. One day the Mughal soldiers succeeded in blowing up one of the bastions by incessantly bombarding the fort with canonballs. Sultan Tana Shah realised the enormity of the situation as there was no way a wall could be constructed overnight. So he thought of a plan. He called his craftsmen and asked them to construct an identical bastion using paper and cloth. Within one night such a realistic, though fake, bastion was erected that the Mughal soldiers were taken aback the next morning. They mistook it for a bastion of stone. Aurangzeb was shocked when he heard this, and this is the bastion which came to be known as the "Paper bastion".'

'A paper bastion!' A lady repeated the phrase, as though trying to go beyond the story to find some deeper meaning.

'Yes, sahib, a paper bastion! It no longer exists, how long can a paper bastion last?'

'The sultan was very clever. But why did his father give him such a strange name? Tana Shah!' someone asked.

'No, sahib, this was not his name. This is what he was affectionately called by his subjects. He could be willful at times . . . a little eccentric, that is all,' the guide replied.

Not a little, a lot! Gopa thought to herself and thought of the incident when a traitor had opened the gate of the fort at night for some rebels. At that very moment, a stray dog started barking and managed to warn everyone. The fort was saved due to its intelligence and loyalty. So, Tana Shah put a gold collar around the neck of the dog and seated it by his side on the throne for many days.

Tana Shah was crazy about dance. That is why he fell in love with the dancer Taramati, who was probably an acrobat apart from being a dancer. She used to come dancing on a high-wire from her palace, Kalamandir, which was a kilometer away, to meet Tana Shah. Her name was indelibly connected with the fort because Tana Shah constructed a mosque in her name – Taramati mosque. Gopa left the group and turned to make her way to the Taramati mosque.

She recollected that once when Tana Shah went on a tour of Kuchipudi village he found that there was a scarcity of water. At his command a well was dug immediately. The local dance which the villagers performed for Tana Shah to show their gratitude was named 'Kuchipudi' by him. The dance still retained its glory, just like the stones of the fort, but Tana Shah, the man who named it was no longer there. Not even in the cemetery of the Qutub Shahi dynasty which is close to Golconda fort! Gopa thought to herself.

Gopa made her way quickly through the lower part of the fort and went inside. She looked up; her gaze went past the Taramati mosque to the Bala Hissar Baradari – the colonnaded pavilion which was built at the top of the hill, adjacent to the blue sky. From this angle she could see the two minarets on the roof of the Baradari soaring towards the sky. Why was it that the thought of the Baradari did not bring the Darbar-e-Aam or the Darbar-e-Khas to her mind but instead reminded her of the two deep wells which lay on the road from the Baradari to Naginbagh? Those deep wells which were now completely dry but were still called wells!

As her gaze slid down the length of the minarets, it was caught by the massive stones below and travelled no further. It was not just her gaze, but the entire mass of the fort which was in the grasp of those boulders. The fort got its name from the Telugu term '*Golla Konda*' meaning the hill of the shepherds. The stones on which it rested were the palms of ancient time, painted with the colours of centuries past.

When Gopa had visited the fort for the first time, the guide, Nizamuddin, told her that the unusual feature of the fort was that it had no foundation. It was supported only by these ancient palms.

'This is something worth seeing, madam…this fort has no foundation. These huge stones have been supporting it for hundreds of years…it was built from the top downwards, not from the ground upwards.'

He continued to speak in his typical Hyderabadi accent while Gopa, trying to shield her eyes from the glare with her right hand, gazed unblinkingly at the boulders. The fort walls had only fallen in places where it was deliberately demolished, otherwise it continued to stand proud in its place, holding onto its past.

In Delhi, many intellectuals and learned men were sacrificed and their heads were buried under the foundations of the Siri Fort, while the Red Fort was built on a groundwork consisting of the corpses of innumerable prisoners. Gopa drew a long breath of relief at the thought that at least there was one fort which was not built on such cruel and inhuman foundations.

Suddenly she shook her head. If only she hadn't studied history! Then, like other ordinary people, she need not have paid attention to subjects like the lack of foundations or what they were based on, and could have detached herself from such brutal images. Mankind has suffered so much at its own hands and this is a sequence which is still continuing in some form or the other, she thought. Somewhere deep inside, we are still the same. This is why we are leaving a historic legacy of inhumanity which is being stored in our subconscious as the foundation of the terrifying fortresses of the future.

Gopa had traversed half the fort but she did not feel like climbing to the top of the hill that day. She thought of going back and once again wandering through the same section of the fort. Whenever she came here in the morning she saw the entire fort at least twice. In any case her very reason for coming to Hyderabad was 'Mission Golconda'. Professor Asthana was writing a research book on Golconda. Gopa had started working for the professor as a research fellow because she needed financial assistance to stay on in Delhi while doing her Ph.D. The professor's work had been interrupted because he had fractured his leg and he had therefore decided to send Gopa to Osmania University to collect some rare material. Gopa couldn't believe her luck! She agreed immediately as this was a perfect opportunity to escape the depressing atmosphere of Delhi and Meerut. But once she came here and saw Golconda she started spending most of her time in the fort and the office of the Archaeological Survey situated next to it, rather than at Osmania University. She liked to visit Golconda because it felt like a wilderness far away from the city.

There was a portico just beyond the entrance to the fort. At its centre was a spot where if one stood and clapped, due to the special technique used in making the twenty-four diamond-cut panels of the high dome, the sound would climb the 380-odd broken stairs and reach the Bala Hissar Baradari, nearly 400 feet up the hill. This helped to warn people that someone was coming in through the lower gate. The same technique had also been used at the spot where some Qutub Shahi sultan used to pronounce judgment after hearing the offences and pleas of criminals. The Sultan would sit in a room on the first floor which was built in such a manner that he could see the criminals but they could not glimpse him. If any prisoner attempted to attack the sultan, the mere touch of his hands on his clothes would echo loudly around the room. Just like memories which send a shiver down the deepest wastelands of the subconscious at the merest touch, diminishing distances of time and space. The loud sound echoing through the room was enough to swing the soldiers into action and get the prisoner arrested. Man has an instinct for self-preservation but the one who wins is either powerful or prosperous. 'Justice' and 'injustice' are mere words, after all!

An ironic smile was etched across Gopa's face. Perhaps it is true that relationships are always incomplete, she thought. The word 'always' drew another parallel smile across her face. Nuanced words, which derive their meaning from their context, are far better than this lifeless, inert word. Only a heart that is wounded begs and pleads, but by the time it does so, the barrier which has grown within the relationship ensures that all such entreaties appear to be addressed to an invisible entity.

During the past two years, whenever Gopa felt the stab of Nikhil's indifference, or when she found him at Ira's, their relationship disintegrated a little more. Gopa would fight with Nikhil, argue, and finally end up in tears over her own helplessness. In response Nikhil would either embroider stories, or try to dab her tears by erecting fences of new promises whose thorns would stab Gopa constantly. Sometimes he would just wrap himself in a cloak of silence and leave. There would be no communication for a few days but with the passage of time Gopa would be forced to get back to him once again. However, the last time Gopa cried, Nikhil's words had dried her tears in an instant, 'Don't you feel we have fallen into a pattern. Crying, cajoling and making up, and you have got used to this pattern.' On hearing the word 'pattern', apart from the tears, a lot else inside Gopa had come to an abrupt end. Perhaps everything. She felt she had been discarded like one of those green coconut shells which lay in piles on the roadside after all the water had been drained out of them. Absolutely empty. As though someone had arrested her on an emotional level using a trickster technique!

The Qutub Shahi guest house inside the fort illustrated a different technique. If two people stood in opposite corners of the room facing the wall and one of them whispered something leaning close to it, the other person could hear him clearly and whisper back an answer. This technique was used to keep a watch on the guests sitting in the room. It is strange that two people could communicate with each other despite sitting so far apart and with their backs to each other, whereas generally despite sitting face to face with others we are unable to convey our meaning to them and our words fall heedlessly to the ground like dry leaves.

After crossing the armoury, Gopa was swiftly walking towards the Bhagmati palace when her steps slowed down as usual. A huge mass of iron weighing 240 kilograms was half-buried in the earth in the corridor. There was a ring embedded in this solid square weight so that it could be lifted. Nizamuddin had told her that any candidate for appointment to the army which protected the fort, had to be able to lift this 240 kilo weight, and people actually did it. Gopa wondered if even one of the seven Qutub Shahi sultans would have been able to lift this weight. Probably not!

We generally use a different yardstick to judge others and so, it is easy to make tall claims but rather difficult to face a tough situation oneself braving a smile! During his Ph.D, the Head of Department had assured Nikhil that he would get a lectureship and that the Head himself would help him to get one. But after the interview the result was totally different from what was promised by the Head. Nikhil became very bitter towards the Head of Department though he went and apologised to him before the next interview was held. This time the wind seemed favourable, but once again the result was negative. Nikhil was really upset and Gopa had to try hard to calm him down. During this time Nikhil met Ira, the daughter of the Head of Department. As the acquaintance evolved into deep friendship Nikhil jettisoned all his past bitterness and took a complete U-turn. Wasn't this a pattern? Gopa felt as though she has been carrying the 240 kilogram weight of iron on her head. God knows since when! Though her work and studies helped her to forget it for a brief while, actually the weight never really moved from its place. It remained half-buried inside her.

Taking off her slippers, Gopa rubbed off the grainy earth which was pinching her feet and moved on. The armoury lay just after the soldiers' barracks. On the right was the area which was known as Naginbagh this day but was earlier called the 'Diamond market'. It was in this market that the traitor Abdullah Khan Pani and his loyal horse were forced to die in agony. The same Aurangzeb with whom Abdullah Khan Pani had colluded by opening the gates of this impregnable fort for the enemies one night, stabbed Khan Pani to death as soon as he entered the fort. Aurangzeb did not even spare the traitor's horse. Lying bloodied in Naginbagh, Abdullah Khan Pani must have seen another wounded corpse lying next to the body of his horse – the carcass of his mutilated ambition which had been betrayed.

Once, in a light-hearted moment, Shirley had listed thirteen synonyms for 'desire' in one breath, as though she was reciting tables, but the word 'ambition' was probably not a part of her list. Desire for instant gratification without any effort and a patient wait – perhaps this was ambition, which Nikhil used to justify in many different ways.

Just a few steps ahead, Gopa crossed a stone parapet on the left and entered the offices of the Qutub Shahi Sultanate of 1672. The offices of Akanna and Madanna, ministers in the reign of the seventh and last sultan Abul Hassan Tana Shah. Just above the parapet which Gopa had crossed were seven-to-eight feet high alcoves which were used to store official documents. Gopa had heard that tall African slaves were employed to arrange and take down the documents. Sitting on the parapet she wondered what the lives of those Africans must have been like. For years many of them had been transported across the seas in ships. Finally, their number increased to such an extent that a separate area was allocated to them in Hyderabad called Habshiguda – the settlement of African slaves, a name by which it was known even to this day.

Whenever these men passed the women's palaces with their heads and eyes lowered, didn't any of the numerous *begums* or beauties of the harem look longingly at them through the reed curtains of these doorless palaces? Gopa thought. Didn't even one of the 101 beauties of Mohammad Quli Qutub Shah wait patiently for him behind the curtains for months and years, despite being part of a large harem?

Gopa moved a few steps and ahead of her was the Bhagmati palace with the Taramati palace next to it. Do we establish or destroy connections with history by addressing ruins as palaces? Do the remnants of a settlement remind us of past sorrows, or of the sorrows of the present? Why don't we remember the joys of the past with the same intensity with which we recall the sorrows? Living in ruins, we listen to and narrate stories of palaces but we feel a throbbing pain inside. Is this the pain of present sorrow or past happiness? Gopa wanted to unravel the knitted rope of the Qutub Shahi dynasty so that each and every strand of it was separated from the other.

Nizamuddin had said that Bhagmati was Taramati's sister, but history said that she was the wife of Muhammad Quli Qutub Shah and Taramati was the beloved of Sultan Tana Shah. There was a gap of almost a hundred years between them. Places, events and human beings are all connected to dates, and so are relationships. Dates and stories of different times can together create an illusion just like the fantasies sometimes created by the conscious and the subconscious.

Gopa was standing in the middle of the Bhagmati palace looking up at its dome. This was the same palace whose walls were once embedded with diamonds and mirrors. As Nizamuddin said, 'Diamonds, mirrors and pearls!' In the evenings, only a tiny little lamp would be lit and its glow would reflect off the diamonds and mirrors like an echo and illuminate the entire palace. After capturing the fort Aurangzeb's soldiers plundered all these diamonds and jewels. When the fort was later handed over to Aurangzeb's son, he wrote to his father requesting that better arrangements be made for his stay. Aurangzeb wondered why his son could not live in such a huge fort. When he made enquiries he got to know that his son did not have enough oil to light up such a large fort. One wonders whether Aurangzeb understood what he had done because if he really had thought better of it he would never have reduced the fort to a wilderness. He would have enjoyed its pleasures, instead.

It is only time which reveals what we have lost because of blind ambition and the anger which grows out of it. But by that time the mirrors, which once reflected the myriad lights of the lamp, are destroyed and abandoned. The connection between the flame and mirror, between a bit of oil and darkness was also a relationship. When Ira, who was three years older to Nikhil, returned to her paternal home after her divorce, Nikhil started visiting her frequently on the pretext of helping her with her Ph.D. And gradually, the oil in the lamp and the brightness of its flame had started diminishing.

Bhagmati, who was the centre of power despite remaining in the background, lived in the palace for quite a long while. Her image had been painted, not with the colours of power but with the rainbow colours of love and art.

Bhagmati was a renowned dancer and lived across the Musi river whereas the thirteen-year-old Muhammad Quli Qutub Shah lived on the opposite shore in the Golconda fort.

He was so madly in love with her that he would swim across the river every day to see her. His father Ibrahim Quli Qutub Shah made many efforts to stop him but finally accepted defeat and built a bridge across the Musi river to ensure his son's safety.

Muhammad Quli Qutub Shah was the third of his father's six children and his mother's first. His mother was princess Bhagirathi of Vijaynagar and a phenomenal amount of gold was distributed to celebrate his birth. After the death of his father Ibrahim, Muhammad Quli Qutub Shah was elected as the sultan by a fake election held under the aegis of a high-ranking official named Rai Rao. As a result of this plot his eldest married brother, who was incarcerated those days for some minor infraction, was declared dead. The second brother, Hussain – a master of logic, philosophy, medicine and astrology – who was away at the time, was not permitted to return to the fort. Somehow, history remained silent about his future existence. After becoming the sultan, Muhammad was married to his brother's fiancée, whom he sent home after a year. Her fault was that the advice given by her Peshwa father to fight against Chand Bibi proved wrong. The fourth and fifth brothers died as soon as Muhammad became the sultan and the sixth brother readily accepted Muhammad's sovereignty and was content to live forgotten in some corner of the fort. So, at the young age of fifteen, Muhammad Quli Qutub Shah became the sultan by unanimous choice.

'The joy of power is so potent and intoxicating.' Gopa remembered these lines which her roommate Shirley used to quote sometimes, adding later, 'These lines are written by Prasad.'

'Prasad…which Prasad?'

'*Arre*, Jaishankar Prasad. You must have studied his poems in school. But how does it matter to you! You are engrossed in your history.' Then after a while she added, 'This is the problem with you history types…you can't see beyond dates and facts…doesn't literature influence history? Isn't it a part of history?'

'Yes, certainly…'

'Then tell me about Jaishankar Prasad!' And seeing Gopa's crestfallen face she had laughed so mischievously that Gopa's irritation had changed into laughter. Shirley, who belonged to Manipur, was doing her Ph.D. in Hindi literature and often, in the evening, she would recite a poem or read out an excerpt from a novel for Gopa. Then she would tease her, 'Now it is your turn! Tell me if there is anything similar in your history but I don't want to hear dates!'

The thought of Shirley brought a slight smile to Gopa's face but the despair in her heart was reflected in her eyes. She had visited Shirley before leaving for Hyderabad. In the garden of the Vimhans Mental Health Hospital patients were sitting on benches surrounded by their relatives. It was visiting time. Shirley was sitting alone and dejected, looking unblinkingly at the setting sun. She knew there was very little possibility of any visitors coming to meet her as all her relatives were in Manipur.

Gopa sat on the bench next to Shirley and touched her shoulder, 'Shirley.'

'Oh, you!' Shirley turned her face, surrounded by a halo of curly hair. 'At least someone has come.'

'How are you?'

'I don't know!' Shirley replied and turned her face towards the setting sun once again. Gopa's palm slid down to Shirley's hand and gently pressed her dejected fingers. Then she withdrew her hand as Shirley said, 'I was sitting in a long-distance train...I got down at some unknown station. I don't know whether I should go on or go back!'

Shirley's eyes were locked onto the sun. In the midst of the surrounding hubbub, the silence on that bench shone like white letters on black paper.

Gopa swept away a black ant crawling on Shirley's kurta but she herself remained inert. Affectionately pushing aside the hair resting untidily on Shirley's shoulder, Gopa addressed her again, 'Shirley.'

'The sun looked just like this one that evening...alone...sad. As though it was leaving civilisation behind and going to a barren world,' Shirley was saying, 'I try very hard to remember which day it was...my memory has become clouded. I think it was the fifteenth of September. On the evening of the fifteenth he took me to Ahmed's den for the first time...' Shirley was sinking silently into the memory of that day.

Gopa knew that Samar, who also belonged to Manipur, was in Shirley's class and that they used to meet at the Majnu-ka-Tila every day after class. Shirley had told her that one day Samar, crushing his cigarette under his feet in the grass, had said, 'This is very boring, coming here every day after class and sitting for hours. How repetitive!'

'So I bore you?' Shirley asked.

'No, that is not true... the two of us alone... how long... there is no kick in this.'

And for this 'kick', Samar took Shirley to Ahmed's den where, together with some friends, Samar and Shirley tasted the intoxicating sweetness of drugs for the first time. The dope which gave Samar the desired kick, made Shirley feel sad and lonely. Samar enjoyed himself with the group but Shirley took more and more drugs to alleviate her loneliness till she reached a stage where her father had to come down from Manipur and admit her, for almost a month, in hospital for de-addiction. Her father had to go back because he had to take care of his business, but Samar, for whom Shirley was still waiting, never came to see her. Why? Was it because of some fear? Because of a feeling of remorse? Or was it just because of his wayward disposition. Whatever the reason, the truth was that sitting alone and sad on a bench in Vimhans Shirley was still lost in the fifteenth of September. She had been admitted to the de-addiction ward to wean her off drugs but was there any ward which could release one from the deadly intoxication of the fifteenth of September or other similar dates?

That day, however, dates had been left outside the Victory gate of the fort and Gopa was sorting through the strands of hair covering the faces of the stories linked to the walls, domes and stones of the fort, trying to see them clearly.

Power or rule or ambition! Muhammad Quli Qutub Shah became the sultan at the age of fifteen but did he really wield power? Wasn't it a puppet show performed to the beats of ambition? Someone is on the stage but the wires are in someone else's hands! Doesn't this often happen? Sultans are manipulated by individuals, by groups, ideologies or by religious compulsions.

Basically, those we think of as 'rulers' are often dancing to the tunes of other people. Rule is like a top which spins with its own momentum but plays a very limited role in determining the beginning and the end of its movement.

Perhaps Nikhil also wanted to improve his life and that was why he targeted Ira so that her HOD father, who was now busy with the preparations for his daughter's wedding to Nikhil, ensured that Nikhil got his appointment as a lecturer even before the marriage culminated. Gopa heaved a long sigh. Who knows who entrapped whom? Ira, who was a divorcee and three years older to Nikhil, must have also spun her own web!

Would Nikhil have taken Ira there? To the same Barista? Did they drink black coffee sitting opposite each other at the same table? Would he have gazed into her eyes for a long time, holding her fingers in his hand? Would he have felt the touch of each of her nails on his cheek? Would he also have said to her, 'We are mutually exclusive!' But he definitely wouldn't have said, 'You still haven't left behind your Meerut mentality. Having a boyfriend doesn't mean getting married to him, nor does being a boyfriend mean wearing a blindfold so that you see only one person in the world… for your entire life… till Nigambodh Ghat, the crematorium.'

If Nikhil hadn't proposed to Ira, wouldn't he have got a job? Perhaps it would have taken a while but he preferred to move ahead faster at the cost of strangling old relationships. Just like Jamshed Quli Qutub Shah, the son of the founder of the dynasty, Sultan Quli Qutub Shah, and the uncle of Muhammad Quli Qutub Shah, who killed his ninety-year-old father because he was impatient to become the ruler! In a civilised, law-abiding society there are specific punishments for killing someone or for attempting to commit suicide, but is there any punishment for breaking somebody's heart?

When Sultan Quli Qutub Shah of Turkmen tribe left Hamadan after facing defeat in 1482 and reached southern India he was a sultan merely in name. His name embodied the dream of his Turkish father, which was achieved in India. On his arrival, Sultan Quli Qutub Shah found employment in the durbar of the Bahamani Sultan. Charismatic, intelligent and adept at swordplay, this Turkish sultan saved the life of the Bahamani Sultan in a battle and was thus promoted and given the title of Qutub-ul-Mulk. The Bahamani Sultan also gifted him the fort of Golconda and made him the governor of Telengana.

At that time the Golconda fort was a mud fort built by the Kakatiya rulers on the stony hill of Mangalavaram 300 years ago. Sultan Quli Qutub Shah clothed the mud walls in stone. Golconda became the capital of Telengana and the Sultan had become its real ruler.

The man who was no longer merely a sultan in name was responsible for laying the foundations of the Qutub Shahi dynasty. In his lust for power, he continued to rule till the age of ninety and by this time his sons were already middle-aged. In the meanwhile one of his sons, Jamshed Quli Qutub Shah, became so impatient to rule that he killed his ninety-year-old father. He also blinded one of his brothers to prevent him from assuming power while another brother, Ibrahim, abandoned Telengana and escaped to Vijaynagar. Jamshed Quli Qutub Shah finally became the undisputed ruler of the fort but couldn't battle the disease which soon consumed him. From the throne to the bier! In the meanwhile, his brother Ibrahim who had fled to Vijaynagar had married princess Bhagirathi. He returned to Golconda and took over the throne. This was the time when Muhammad Quli Qutub Shah, the lover of Bhagmati, was born.

Muhammad Quli Qutub Shah had four wives and at least a hundred other women in his harem, yet, for a long time, he had no children. Finally, his favourite wife Bhagmati bore him his only child, a daughter named Hayat Bakshi Begum. Why did this happen? Why was it that his other wives and the beauties of his harem could not give him this joy?

The love story and the marriage of the dancer Bhagmati and Muhammad Quli Qutub Shah envelop the history of that time like a rosy cloud. Don't these romantic clouds scattered through history and civilisation give the fairer sex the leisure of consoling themselves with soap bubbles? Gopa thought. And these romantic bubbles transform some people into Shirley. Shirley, who was sitting on the bench in the park at Vimhans, waiting for someone to visit her!

When Muhammad used to swim across the Musi river to meet Bhagmati he was only thirteen years old while Bhagmati, a famous dancer, was much older to him. Their love affair carried on for many years. During that time Muhammad was married a few times and the number of inhabitants of his harem also increased largely. Then he married Bhagmati and received the gift of his only child from her. Thereby, didn't she also give the sultan the opportunity to appear as a 'complete man' in front of his subjects? This may have been the reason why Muhammad Quli Qutub Shah rewarded her by naming the new settlement built to accommodate the growing population of Golconda fort, 'Bhagnagar'. When Bhagmati's name was later changed to Hyder Mahal, the new city was renamed Hyderabad.

Was this just love? What about the other wives? Why did

he only have a child with Bhagmati who, because of her age and her life as a public dancer, must have been more experienced and worldly-wise? Doesn't history often elevate love stories to the level of fairy tales?

In fairy stories rabbits jump about on the moon and old women work at their spinning wheels. Gopa's life had also been illuminated by one evening which had been like a fairy tale. Once Nikhil had taken her to Agra to show her the Taj Mahal. Gopa had expressed a desire to see the Taj by the moonlight and Nikhil had decided to indulge her. They had gone to Agra telling everyone in the hostel that they were going to Meerut. After seeing the Taj, soaked in the glow of the moonlight, Nikhil had escorted Gopa back to her room and stayed on. That night, the darkness within Gopa's body had tried to soak up the feeling of completeness which was touching her heart like drops of moonlight. A touch which still lingered somewhere around her, even now. She had filled the courtyard of her life with the light of Nikhil's love and he had decorated it with patterns that made Gopa shiver when she saw them in the mirror after he left. She had wanted to look at them, only them. This joy had blossomed again, during lazy afternoons and shy evenings. But how can fairy tales become the verities of life?

Hayat Bakshi Begum was the lifeline of her mother Bhagmati. Was this merely because she was Bhagmati's only child? Hayat Bakshi Begum was betrothed to the prince of Iran, who arrived in Golconda with a huge entourage and waited for six years for the marriage to be solemnised. During this period an engagement also happened, but after six years the prince was sent back to Iran with complete honour, loaded with many gifts and Hayat Bakshi Begum was married to her father's nephew. Why? Gopa felt this was a deliberate move in the game of power which was played with great intelligence by Bhagmati. Would Bhagmati have allowed her daughter to go away to Iran? Was her relationship with Hayat Bakshi Begum just the natural affectionate one between a mother and her daughter, or was Hayat Bakshi Begum also the key to power?

Muhammad Quli Qutub Shah passed away at the age of forty-six and Hayat Bakshi Begum's husband became the new sultan. Later she herself ruled for a while after her husband's death. If these events had not occurred would Bhagmati, the dancer who became a queen, have been able to live in such grandeur in her Bhagmati palace? Would the palace still have been known by the same name? Would the love story of Muhammad Quli Qutub Shah and Bhagmati have continued to transport us to the cloudy realms of romance?

What are relationships? Relationships which survive birth and re-birth! Relationships which have names and others which are nameless! Someone like Taramati has her name associated with a sacred place like a mosque while someone like Muhammad Quli Qutub Shah's first wife found herself sent back to her paternal home after a year of unconsummated marriage. Gopa suddenly shivered. What had happened to her? Why did she come to the fort everyday and then lose herself in its history? Why was her grip on her thoughts, her mind weakening? Was she also like Shirley…the thought brought a deathly cold shiver. No, Nikhil said that Shirley was over-sensitive. But why? It may be true that I have, what Nikhil calls, a small-town mentality, but Shirley was educated at Mayo College in Ajmer, Gopa thought. Even in Delhi she was considered to be a fairly liberal-thinking girl. Then why did she fall prey to depression? A bat flew over Gopa's head, startling her. When she looked up she saw several bats suspended from the dome. They may bite! As soon as this thought hit her, Gopa felt as though hundreds of bats were stuck to her body. She got up, dusted her clothes and sat down once again at a short distance away. She wondered if this dusting of her clothes was becoming a mannerism. Didn't she often dust her clothes like this when she wanted to free herself from unwanted thoughts? Bats could hurt the body but what could she do about those thoughts which haunted her very being like ghosts. They clung to her like bats, bats of the distant and recent past. 'Do I also need counselling? No! I have to get a grip on myself,' Gopa decided. 'I am a student of history. I should be objective. Why am I trying to dig up the foundations of these stories and legends?'

History was meant to be objective, but why did it play the song of Muhammad Quli Qutub Shah and Bhagmati's love? And why the holes of the flute got clogged while playing the elegy for the real heir to the throne, Hussain Quli Qutub Shah, who was Muhammad's elder brother? Was Hussain put to death? Did he run away to Iran? Why did this happen? Hussain was very talented and learned, then why didn't the courtiers choose him? Perhaps he was too sober and serious. He had a vision, the ability to take his own decisions. So he would never have been a puppet in the hands of the courtiers. Where did his fiancée, who was later married to his younger brother, go after she had been rejected by her husband? Did this unfortunate lady ever meet her former fiancée? Our objective history is silent about all this. The deep silence of a dark wilderness! History is about victors; or rather it is they who have it written. The losers are like the ruined bastion of Golconda which cannot even become memorials!

Muhammad Quli Qutub Shah was elected by the courtiers under the tutelage of Rai Rao. Muhammad's mother was the princess of Vijaynagar, so the ties between Vijaynagar and the Golconda fort and Telengana must have been strengthened once her son became the Sultan. Perhaps the Hindu courtiers chose the son of a Hindu mother as the sultan to protect their own interests and set an example of communal unity! Who knows what the reason was, but innumerable innocents were sacrificed to shore up the foundations of this fortress of communal unity. What was this? The politics of religion, or the religion of politics? It is so strange that while politics does require the help of religion, even religion is unable to survive without the support of politics!

It is an old saying that dcath takes us to the place where we are destined to die, Gopa thought to herself. Ever since she could remember, Nikhil had been somewhere close by. His family lived on the first floor of Gopa's house, so the children shared the same courtyard. Nikhil helped Gopa with her studies since her childhood. By the time she appeared for her class tenth board exams Nikhil had already gone to Delhi to study. But he would help her whenever he came home on weekends. Gopa fared so well in her boards that not just her family and friends but the whole of Meerut was stunned. None of Gopa's sisters had scored so well, so everyone was convinced that her brilliant performance was the result of Nikhil's efforts. The Gopa hibernating inside her body gradually awoke. After class twelve she also left for Delhi, at Nikhil's urging, to do her B.A. Her excellent marks helped open the doors of the hostel for her. Nikhil stayed in another hostel in Delhi. He was doing his M.Phil. What if she had listened to her mother and continued to study in Meerut like her sisters?

Gopa wondered. No one wishes to go to one's final destination; it is *death* which draws one to that place. Nikhil, who was once like a strong banyan tree for Gopa, had become just a memory. Memories continue to have a life of their own just as death ripens alongside life.

The life of the last sultan of the Qutub Shahi dynasty, Abul Hassan Tana Shah, was a similar convoluted story. He might have experienced the religion of politics and the politics of religion so closely that he was totally disenchanted and left the fort to live under the guidance of the Sufi saint Shah Raju. Abul Hassan was a distant relative of the ruling sultan but as he had no heir this Sufi descendant of the Qutub Shahis was called back to the fort and placed on the throne.

Tana Shah reigned for fourteen years during which he had to continually face threats from Aurangzeb. The Moghul kept trying to conquer the Golconda fort but was unsuccessful. Finally when the traitor Abdullah Khan Pani opened the gates of the fort for Aurangzeb, Tana Shah was imprisoned and taken to Aurangabad where he spent the last fourteen years of his life. Fourteen years of rule and fourteen years of imprisonment!

It is said that Tana Shah remained absolutely calm when Aurangzeb's soldiers came to arrest him. He politely asked the Moghul commander Ruhullah Khan to be seated and requested him for a little time to say his prayers. After his *namaz*, Tana Shah invited the enemy soldiers to join him for a meal and then bid adieu to the fort, and to power.

How could Tana Shah remain so calm and balanced even at the moment of the destruction of the Qutub Shahi rule? Perhaps because of his Sufi bent of mind. His Sufi mind could fathom the thought processes of power-hungry minds very well. That is the reason why he had a paper bastion made to replace the wall and battlements of the fort which had been destroyed.

What is a paper bastion? An artistic creation or a mirage? The illusion of a stone wall. A wall which does not exist in reality but appears that it does. A curtain constructed overnight which is ephemeral, transient and which can provide satisfaction only for a brief while. For a moment Gopa descended into the depths of her being. In her mind she heard, 'Paper bastion that is, love.'

'*Arre*, you are here alone in the dark! It is time to close the fort for visitors,' Nizamuddin's voice startled Gopa.

She stood up, 'I was about to leave.' As she moved towards the exit she suddenly thought of a story. She tried to push it aside and not think of anything. She just wanted to get out of the fort as early as possible but she knew it was not possible for her to avoid these thoughts any longer. For the past few months irrelevant incidents or events would suddenly come to her mind. Do disrupted relationships also lead to a disjointing of thoughts? The story accompanied her, even in its abbreviated form.

A child sliced an earthworm into two with a knife. When his mother noticed this she was upset and asked him, 'Why did you do this?'

Looking at the worm, the child replied in a dejected voice, 'It was alone; I just wanted it to have a friend.'

Nizamuddin's voice came from afar, 'Goodbye. May God be with you!' He was using the dangerous shortcut to get out of the fort. Gopa knew the path crossed the Qutub Shahi cemetery which lay outside the fort. As though death was waiting just beyond the walls of the citadel!

The darkness was deepening, spreading its wings over the fort. The shadow of tall trees added depth to the darkness outside and desolation was oozing through the cracks in the ceiling of her mind. Gopa walked on, and as she trampled the red earth her steps made a squeaking sound which cut through the silence all around. The feeling that there was a broken bastion in the distance halted her steps for a moment. She felt as though she could remember a face but not its name, or she could recall the name but not the face. What difference did it make? There was a similar lack of completeness in either. Suddenly a whirlpool of echoes arose in the dry, dejected, dark well of her mind – paper bastion. She walked ahead with leaden steps because the paper bastion had collapsed completely but somewhere within a half-cut worm was creeping about on its rubble.

Pandemic

Space is nothing but void. There is no concept of directions, objects, soil or air. The 'supreme' light has no existence alone. It only acquires an identity when it focuses on an object. When light is reflected off that object, it becomes visible to us and the light gains its existence. If there is an object in space and light falls on it, then only that object is visible to us in that void; nothing else, only because the light has been reflected off it.

Who knows why this principle of physics came to Madhav's mind at the instant when he was being jolted along in the car. Aren't memories like light? And isn't the past like those objects off which memory is reflected? Sitting next to him, Jyoti wanted to make use of every opportunity to pass on information. Afraid that in the flood of information which characterised the present age, her Siddhi would be left behind the 'finishing line'.

'Look, this is Khadakwasla, Khadakwasla village…' Jyoti was determined to acquaint the thirteen-year-old Siddhi with every bit of information about the place.

Madhav remembered the time before Siddhi was born, when Jyoti used to make fun of parents who had the same habit. She had once narrated Rabindranath Tagore's story – 'Parrot'. It was about the unfortunate parrot who was stuffed so full of facts and figures that it collapsed. *Information in, breath out!* At such times Madhav often felt that Siddhi was reluctant to open her mouth while Jyoti was busy trying to ram more and more information down her throat.

After their marriage it had been quite a while before Siddhi was born. Why did Jyoti's attitude change immediately after giving birth to her child? Why did she herself turn into the principal of the story, 'Parrot'? She even forgot that Siddhi was no longer a small child but thirteen years old. And that too, not an Indian teenager but one who had grown up in America where children of her age often lived in their own world, away from their parents.

The words of knowledge were buffeting against the wind and sound of the car engine and couldn't reach Madhav. He muttered to himself, 'Shove it down... shove it down...'

'Mama, I know it! I read all this when I checked out information about Pune on the internet.'

'But you might not know that in Khadakwasla...'

'Oh please, let it be,' Siddhi's words suddenly brought Jyoti's barrage to a halt, 'Look, the rush of water from that dam is so forceful. Great!'

Travelling in the opposite direction of the one being traversed by the car, the light of Madhav's memories shone on the year 1962 – the year of the Chinese aggression. That was the year the dam in Khadakwasla had suddenly been breached and the city of Poona had been submerged. At that time Madhav used to teach in a nearby village in the primary school which had 'Zila Parishad

School' written on a board outside. He felt as though the rush of his memories was like the breached dam of Khadakwasla rather that merely a light illuminating the past.

When the car moved ahead Madhav put his hand out of the window and pointed far away saying, 'That is Khadakwasla village where we used to go some twenty-five years ago...to catch mosquitoes.' Madhav was speaking to himself, acquainting his present with his distant past but Siddhi caught his words, 'Mosquitoes! Here...so far away?'

'Yes, there were millet fields here at that time...now there are restaurants and hotels everywhere...'

'What could we do, sahib? Money attracts money. The farmers sold their lands and hotels and lodges were constructed on them. What could fields give them? Barely enough to stave off their hunger and clothe them. That's all! Hotels earn money.' The driver of the car also started moving back in time.

'Did you find the most mosquitoes near ponds?' Siddhi's curiosity was aroused.

'No, in houses or near cow-sheds.'

'What? In cow-sheds?'

'Where cows and buffaloes stay.'

'So you used to go into those...those cow-sheds?' Siddhi was incredulous.

'Yes, we had to go, and that too in the evening because the Malaria mosquitoes only come out after dark and remain active all night,' Madhav replied.

'And you also remained active along with them in the cow-sheds all night!' Siddhi's voice was full of wonder.

'Once your papa was so active in these cow-sheds that he even forgot my birthday party.' Jyoti had also retreated into the past.

'Yes, that night I was looking after some 500 mosquitoes which I had caught from some village nearby and sitting in the dark I was imagining the world war that was going to happen between your mother and me the next day,' Madhav added in an abashed tone.

'500 mosquitoes. Oh my god!'

'We used to collect more than 500-1000 mosquitoes at one go sometimes.'

'Once you told me that you used an instrument similar to a snake charmer's flute to capture these mosquitoes.'

'It wasn't a flute, it was a glass instrument shaped like one. When you pull in your breath the mosquitoes get sucked in. There is rubber attached to both ends of the pipe and its centre is quite round, the mosquitoes get collected into that fat, round part. The end from which you breathe in is covered by a fine mesh so that the mosquitoes don't get into your mouth.'

'Then you used to take the mosquitoes to the lab the next morning?'

'Yes, and there we would separate the different races... I mean species.' As he uttered these words Madhav thought to himself that man had managed to spread his consciousness of race in mosquitoes as well.

'It must be easier to study the mosquitoes after separating them into different species?' Jyoti asked.

'Yes, and sometimes we would even discover new species of mosquitoes while doing this.'

As Siddhi's memory travelled back in time an innocent smile spread across her face. 'Papa, do you remember when I was small you told me that a friend of yours brought a rat from Ladakh which was so huge that people used to come just to look at it. And you people had also given it a name.'

'Name...yes, we did call him something.' The sparkle in Madhav's eyes gradually dimmed as he recalled another incident when he had discovered a new sub-species of mosquito at a famous tourist spot. Generally any new species of mosquito or rat, etc., was named after the place where it was discovered. But the town administration refused to permit this species of mosquito to be named after the town. They were afraid that this might lead to a scare and discourage tourists from visiting their town. There was an exchange of letters and phone calls among important people. The poor mosquito remained nameless for many days. Finally, an abbreviation was used and the world became acquainted with the new sub-species. Madhav for the first time realised that power, influence and money could play such an important role even in the naming of a mosquito.

Names have their own politics. Seventeenth century metal plates discovered during excavations reveal that at that time Pune was ruled by Rashtrakutas and it was known as 'Punya Vishya' or 'Punaka Vishya' which meant 'the pure region'. After around two centuries the name changed to 'Punaka Vadi' and 'Punaka Desh'. Later it was called 'Kasbe Pune'. After conquering the city Aurangzeb named it 'Muhiyabad' after his grandson. On the one hand people say 'what's in a name?' and on the other they keep changing the names of places.

'Papa, those bats...what do you call them? A very funny name...'

'*Chamgadad*!'

'Yes, *chamgadad*! You used to catch them here as well, didn't you?' Siddhi asked from the back seat.

Madhav replied turning back a little, 'Do you know bats have amazing communication skills and discipline. Just like school kids!'

'Like school kids!' Siddhi repeated, giggling.

'Bats live together but they leave their caves in the evening always in a group. Each species leaves in a separate group followed ten or fifteen minutes later by another species, and then a third group, like children from different classes coming out one by one during the sports period.'

'Ha, ha, ha…' Siddhi laughed, but suddenly turned serious. 'But you people used to capture them.'

'Yes, but we used to release them again after taking their blood samples,' Madhav said, dispelling Siddhi's gloom a little.

'Here we are! We have reached Singh Garh,' the driver announced as he parked the car. Jyoti bought slices of green tamarind from a Marathi girl sitting on the stony steps of the fort and passed them on to Siddhi along with a bit of salt.

Madhav bought some green gram and told the driver, 'What are you going to do here alone? Come along and see the fort.' He passed him a fistful of gram.

'Why is everyone eating while climbing up the stairs? Some people are eating cucumbers…' Siddhi asked as she enjoyed the sour taste of the green tamarind.

'Baby, you don't feel thirsty while climbing if you eat something,' the driver replied.

After climbing up the uneven steps of the fort and crossing two doorways made of stone, Siddhi saw a small temple. The temple of Goddess Mukai. She stopped at the door. Just then she heard Jyoti's voice, 'Madhav, look someone is selling *jhunka bhakri* there. Let's eat some.' Everyone turned around to look at the place to which Jyoti was pointing. There was a faint smile on Madhav's face. 'Come on, we have come here after so many years,' Jyoti repeated tugging at Madhav's arm.

'Sahib, you have something to eat. I will just be back,' the driver said and walked off towards 'Rasvanti Greh', perhaps to drink some sugarcane juice.

As he ate *jhunka bhakri* (millet bread) and curd curry sitting in the small restaurant built at the side of the fort, Madhav had a strange feeling as if someone was being given the opportunity to relive the bygone moments of his life. After completing his M.Sc. in geology from Pune he had taken admission in the Ph.D programme and joined the Virus Research Organisation as a project fellow. The job was temporary but the experience was permanent. He worked there for five years and during that period he visited Khadakwasla and villages around Singh Garh many times.

At that time, Singh Garh was merely an old fort for him built on a hill twenty-five kilometers away from the city. But now he knew that the fort had always been of great importance for Pune. Mohammad Tughlaq had also come to Singh Garh. For the Shah of Bijapur, Singh Garh was an invaluable treasure. It was known as Kondhana fort. It was Shivaji who named it Singh Garh. When Shivaji conquered it the Shah of Bijapur was so enraged that he imprisoned Shivaji's father. Ultimately the Mughal emperor Shah Jahan in Delhi intervened on Shivaji's behest and had his father released. But Shivaji lost Singh Garh once again to the Mughals because of some treaty and had to bide his time to regain his favourite fort.

'This tastes a bit strange,' Siddhi said. 'Papa, why don't you get the stuff that those people are eating?'

Madhav looked at the table next to them and told the young waiter, 'Get us a plate of *kanda bhaji* and two of curd.' The boy quickly came back with a plate of onion fritters and black earthen bowls of curd.

'It is good that we left this place and settled abroad. In any case it is very difficult to come back and settle down once again in the same way.'

Madhav did not respond to this statement of Jyoti. He thought to himself that it wasn't so easy to leave behind the memories of the past.

Shivaji had also returned. He was fuelled by the desire to conquer Singh Garh – the Lion fort – once again. That was why he had sent a message on the cold wintry night of the fourth of February (1670) to his dear childhood friend and colleague Tanaji Malusare to attack Singh Garh. At that time Tanaji was celebrating his son's engagement. Shivaji knew that apart from him, only Tanaji could find his way through those valleys, chasms and hilly trails. And the general left for the fort with his soldiers as soon as he received Shivaji's message.

The Mughals had entrusted the protection of that impregnable fort to Rajput Udaybhan. There was a function in the fort that night so all the soldiers were busy in the celebrations. Tanaji suddenly launched an attack with his 300 soldiers. He tied the one-and-a-half foot long, giant Iguanas to one end of a rope ladder and swung it up towards the battlements of the fort. In keeping with its nature, the Iguanas clung so strongly to the wall that they could not be moved. The soldiers then climbed up ladder. The Rajputs were so intoxicated that it took them some time to prepare themselves and respond to the attack. In the meanwhile the Marathas under the leadership of Tanaji, had already moved into the fort. A fierce battle took place in which Tanaji first lost his arm and then his life. Fire signals were used to send a message to Shivaji at Rajgarh, 900 miles away, to inform him that the fort had been taken. Shivaji came immediately and expressing his sorrow at the loss of his dear friend said, 'We have won the fort but lost the lion.'

Shivaji's mother Jijabai was anguished by the death of Tanaji and found it hard to come to terms with it. She summoned Tulsidas Charan from Pune and ordered him to write an epic poem about the brave exploits of Tanaji. And thus Tanaji became immortal through these songs and verses.

It is only a few chosen martyrs who are lucky enough to be remembered and sung about centuries after they have passed away. Not everyone is lucky enough to have a poem written about him!

Now Madhav was standing at the corner of the hill on which the fort was situated. When he glanced down he realised that the valley below was just like the chasm deep inside him whose depths sometimes stopped the blood flow in his veins, leaving him in a state of limbo. Only the tingling in his hands and feet reminded him that he existed. There was a pond right in the middle of the valley below. As Madhav stared at it he could see the blurred outlines of a face. Keshav's face. Keshav with his black curly hair; the way he was around eighteen years ago. If Keshav was alive today, would he look like this? he thought. No. His hair would have grayed by now.

How and why do some incidents occur in life? When they do, life does not even give one the chance to think about them. Invisible hands seem to guide these events, Madhav thought to himself as he looked at Keshav's static face in the still water. It is just the play of the visible and the invisible. We can see only as far as the light illuminates events, the rest remains invisible and unknown.

'Papa, fireplace!' Siddhi was calling out from the platform built at the edge of the hill.

'Soldiers must have kept watch sitting in this picket, fighting the cold.' It was Jyoti's voice.

'Wow!' Siddhi looked at the fireplace with wonder-filled eyes. She went close and bent down as though to warm her hands at the fire. 'How romantic!' she delightedly said.

As Madhav walked up to them he thought that the lives of those soldiers must have been extremely tough. Covered from head to toe by the shadows of death sent to them by those hankering for power and authority. Each moment would have been like a threat. If they were attacked from outside they would face death at the hands of the enemy and if they made the barest error of judgment, they would be killed by their own people. However, those in power would rarely have waited for them to commit any mistake to jeopardise their lives. Even the idiosyncrasies of the rulers would have been enough for that. And the brave yet helpless struggle of such a soldier appears 'romantic' to us today.

What was Tanaji's life? Would this generation call it 'romantic' as well? It is impossible to forget what he did for his friend Shivaji. Was Shivaji merely a friend? Wasn't he also Tanaji's leader? And Keshav? Keshav was also his friend as well as his boss – a colleague in a true sense. And yet he had tried to run away from even the memories of his colleague and friend. Oh! Madhav gently shook his head. What had happened to him that day? Why was his mind wandering to the past? It felt as though his thoughts were also climbing up and down the stairs of an old fort.

Madhav worked in Pune for five years to do his Ph.D in entomology. When he got the offer of a permanent job as an entomologist in a research institution he immediately left his hometown and settled down in Bangalore. Dr Keshav Madhavan was his boss. He had met Jyoti in Keshav's room for the first time and they had married after a few months.

Madahv was still new in the office but ever since he joined he used to find Keshav quite lost and silent. His silence would make Madhav feel constantly uneasy. Sometimes Madhav would pick up his tiffin and land up in Keshav's room during the lunch hour. Initially the depressing atmosphere was unbearable for both of them but gradually they got used to it. Keshav would wait for Madhav to come and Madhav would try to wind up his work quickly so that he could share his lunch with Keshav. But was it merely the lunch? Perhaps not. It may have been the blue halo of that brilliant academic record holder – Keshav – which attracted Madhav; which made him feel uneasy but also appeared to be the only means of deliverance from that unease.

Now Madhav had even started visiting Keshav at his home in the evening sometimes. On one of these evenings Keshav told him that he wasn't really quiet at moments when he appeared to be silent. He was constantly conversing with that one dream he nurtured deep in his heart – the dream of making some new contribution to the world of medicine; some new discovery. This dream was the basis of his very being. Then after a while he had said, 'Think of it as my alter-ego... sometimes I wonder if I would exist without it! What would I live for!'

'Dream!' This was the only word Madhav had managed to utter after jostling with all the words that filled his mind.

'Yes, Madhav…you can just write it on paper today! I will show you how I make my dream come true.' Then he had turned a little serious and said, 'But I need your cooperation for this.'

'Mine?'

'Yes, such great enterprises can't be accomplished single-handedly. They are a result of the honest efforts of many individuals. I will show the way.'

Each pore of Madhav's being was filled with a strange sense of excitement. 'We are all with you.' He put his hand on Keshav's hand, 'I am with you. Now this is not just your dream but everyone's. If there is any major discovery in the field of science it will benefit not just our own community but the whole world.'

Keshav's eyes were misty. He pressed Madhav's hand lightly.

Keshav's dream and his words had induced vigour in Madhav's life as well. Work had gained a new dimension thereon. His family and his own self slowly drifted to the background. His life was but the dreams of Keshav hovering over his subconscious and rest being the daily chores, the research lab, office, phone, computer and internet.

Once, on a dark evening they met over a glass of beer for discussion. Keshav was looking despondent and Madhav asked him, 'What happened? Are you anxious about something?'

'Nothing new!' Keshav answered briefly.

'Why didn't you have any beer today? Should I pour some whisky for you? Your mood elevator!' Madhav added, smiling.

'No, friend, it is OK!' Somehow everything appeared meaningless to Keshav.

'What?'

'Why is this happening?' Keshav appeared to be in a different world.

'What?' Madhav wanted to know.

'That it doesn't make any difference to anyone anymore...'

'It isn't making any difference to you, either! Look, you are drinking beer instead of whisky.' Madhav seemed to have decided not to take anything seriously.

'Stop joking!'

This time Madhav was silent.

'Sometimes I remember some incident and I keep thinking about it, and the more I think the more I feel a sense of emptiness inside...as though I am standing all alone in my lab in the quiet of the night; there are no instruments in the lab, no computers. I stand there, bewildered, in the middle of those four empty walls surrounded by the sharp smell of the lab which quickly penetrates my brain. Sometimes I feel there is too little oxygen...as though my heart has missed a beat.'

'Keshav,' Madhav sounded worried, 'what is going through your mind right now?'

'I was thinking that was the disease that spread through those villages situated near the shores of Kerala, really plague? Or was it something else? Why didn't we ever reach a conclusion which was credible?'

'This is an old story. I was in Pune at the time. Today all that...' Madhav looked questioningly at Keshav.

'Think about it, Madhav. An epidemic spreads through two villages in Kerala close to the jungles...' Keshav's voice became stronger.

'Yes, I remember...that was plague.' Madhav wanted to get to the real point quickly.

'How can you say it was the plague?' Keshav asked abruptly, startling Madhav.

'It was plague, everyone said it.'

'Who said it?'

'All the reports.'

'Official reports and our media, that's all! Who else?'

'What do you mean?'

'I mean that whatever is said or claimed is not necessarily the truth.'

'Not necessarily but…' Madhav tried to explain but Keshav was only listening to the voice of his mind.

'When I think of or hear such things, my heart sinks. I even lose interest in my work. I feel like smashing my dream. Throw it out of my life, my consciousness. Everything else is rubbish…just rubbish.'

'What happened? Why are you talking like this?'

Keshav had sunk down further into the sofa. His voice emerged after a while as though it was coming out of a deep hole, 'There was such a terrible earthquake in that jungle in Kerala that year that the jungle and all the villages nearby were completely destroyed.'

'Yes, I know…' Madhav tried to say something but Keshav's mind had drifted somewhere far away.

'People had become homeless. The foundations of schools, post-offices, dispensaries, government offices had all been shaken. People started living in camps.'

Keshav waited and then continued after a moment, 'The sympathies of the entire world were with us because of the earthquake. Every country wanted to help us generously. They said, "take anything." '

Keshav took a deep breath and then gestured with his hands, 'Take this money, take clothes, grain…anything. But our government said with confidence, "Thank you very much. We can manage." All the countries complimented us.'

'Finish the last sip,' Madhav gestured towards the glass.

Keshav picked up the glass and drained it saying, 'At this moment a big country comes forward, puts a friendly hand on our country's shoulder, and says, "Friend, it is true that you are capable. You can look after your own people. We appreciate your sentiments but listen to what we have to say." Such a large nation treating us with such friendliness, our country proudly replies, "So what do you want to say?" The big country says, "Look, you have taken care of all the important things but the people who are living in camps are not troubled as much by the lack of food as they are by mosquitoes. You can ask your workers if you don't believe us." '

'What could the workers say? They had also pointed out the problems caused by mosquitoes.' Madhav wanted to move ahead.

'Then that big country said, "So listen to us, brother. Even if you don't need anything else take some anti-mosquito spray from us free of cost. At least people will be able to sleep in peace." Our government saw nothing objectionable in this suggestion,' Keshav added.

'And we took the spray,' Madhav completed the story.

'Yes, and thousands of spray bottles reached the camps providing relief to the people and the workers.' Keshav saw Madhav filling the glass and kept looking at him for a few moments.

Then he leaned his head back and closed his eyes. Madhav took a sip from his glass and asked Keshav, 'So, that is the end of the story?'

'No, the story is going to start now,' Keshav said, opening his eyes. 'You know that just a month or so later a terrible epidemic spread through that village and its symptoms were very similar to that of plague?'

'So you are trying to say that it wasn't the plague . . .?'

'Let me finish what I am saying. We all know that during the plague ninety percent of the people get high fever and nodules in their thighs. Only in ten percent cases the germs of plague reach the lungs causing pneumonia.' Madhav listened silently as Keshav continued, 'You know those ninety percent can be given some medical care but for the remaining ten percent there is no cure. Death is certain; a helpless death.' Then placing emphasis on each and every word he said, 'And the plague which spread in these camps was of the ten percent variety. But why? Tell me why?'

'Yes, that's true but who knows why?' Madhav wondered.

'Why did this happen for the first time in the history of this epidemic? And even more strange was the fact that despite this disease being associated with the death of rats, not even a single dead rat was found anywhere in this area. Why? Then where did the plague germs come from?'

'What are you trying to say?'

'This...this was the question which people in important positions in our government institutions asked our bewildered scientists who were wondering why this epidemic was being called 'plague'. How did it appear without any rats? They wanted a proper investigation to be conducted but no one listened to them.'

Keshav got up, turned the fan faster, and sat down. Madhav was still trying to gauge the real meaning of Keshav's words when he heard him say, 'Some scientists popular with the government said that those creating a hue and cry were merely inexperienced. They were taking the written word as the *Bible*. They claimed that thousands of dogs had been killed in those villages during a cleanliness crusade, which interfered with the eco-cycle and led to the epidemic.'

'So what was the real reason?'

'I don't know but at this time that big nation approaches us again and says, "We can help you solve this problem." Our country asks, "How?" It replies, "Let us take some blood samples of the affected people. We will test them in our labs and give you the answers. You don't have the same facilities, after all." Our country replied, "You have already helped us, why don't you let us do this ourselves." The big country tries to persuade us saying this is beyond our abilities but for some reason our country doesn't agree. At this juncture another white country approaches us saying, "Don't give them the samples if you don't want to. Give them to us. You really don't have the proper facilities." And our country agrees. Thousands of blood samples are sent by air to that white country and then disaster strikes.'

'Disaster!' Madhav exclaimed.

'Yes, the lab of that country had to be shut down due to some serious technical problem. It was not advisable to leave the blood samples out for so many days. All our efforts were going to be wiped out. Then that white country asked us to give the blood samples to the big country.'

'The blood samples did go there.' Madhav nodded his head in agreement.

'The blood samples reached the big country. They were examined and our government was informed that it was the plague. Our naïve government immediately made the announcement saying the matter did not need to be discussed any further. The media took up the work on behalf of the government and spread the news around like a cloud of mosquitoes. A few restless doctors and scientists like me kept making noises about this unscientific and illogical end to a scientific issue.' Keshav's voice became softer, 'Government doctors and scientists couldn't say anything after the official announcement. Gradually the matter was forgotten, or that is what we thought.'

'What do you mean?' asked Madhav.

'I mean that there was another country which was keeping an eye on all these developments,' Keshav replied.

'I didn't know about this.'

'Yes, and after a few years it released a report which stated that the epidemic was not the plague at all. It was not a natural disaster; it was caused by germs contained in the sprays provided to us by the big country to kill mosquitoes.'

'What!' Madhav found in hard to believe.

'The big country wanted to test the germs it had created for bio-chemical warfare. The test was successful. The poor people of our country were used as guinea pigs,' Keshav revealed.

'What are you saying!'

'I am telling the truth. This other country was neither our friend nor a friend of the human race. Its only regret was that it had created a similar microbe for bio-chemical warfare but had been unable to find any guinea pigs whereas the big country had cleverly succeeded in its attempts.'

'Oh no!'

'The big country is very happy because it now possesses bio-chemical weapons which have been successfully tested and the chapter has been closed in our country. We cannot even discuss it because the government has stated that it was "natural plague" and nothing else.'

Keshav became silent. Just then the phone rang. Madhav glanced at Keshav's face and then got up and picked up the phone. He told the caller that Keshav would call him back after ten-fifteen minutes. Keshav looked at Madhav gratefully as though he was saying, 'Thank you, Madhav, always be with me.'

'But today…at this time…this old story?' Madhav asked as he sat down once again.

'Yes, I had kept some reports of the new country with me. Today I came across them when I opened my almirah and my heart…' Keshav's voice was muffled; tears streaming down his face.

'But why did the government do this?' Madhav asked after a while.

'I don't know. The more I think about it, the more disturbed I feel. My mind gets confused and I can't reach any conclusion.'

'Do you think this happened because of centre-state tensions?'

'Why? Why not because of the pressure of another country?'

'Another country? But who?' Madhav was perplexed.

'The same big country. Doesn't this entire thing seem to be a well-thought out scheme?'

'But our country had refused to give them the blood samples. It was just because of circumstances…'

'This may be true or may be not.' Keshav didn't let Madhav complete his sentence.

'What do you mean?'

'Maybe the government was just trying to pull wool over our eyes? A terrible, cruel joke played on the helpless and unaware people…it is just being inhuman.' Keshav sank further into the sofa.

Siddhi's voice pulled Madhav out of his memories in which he had been lost. 'Did this fort collapse on its own, or did someone bring it down?' Siddhi was asking, looking at the crumbling stone walls of the fort.

'Must have collapsed by itself, baby. Who has the time to sit and break it!' the driver answered her.

With the memory of Keshav's story about the plague still lingering in his mind Madhav recalled the reference in Tilak's biography, to the plague that hit Poona in 1897 during the time of the British. The flames of the epidemic spread as far as Bombay. There was no medication available to stop the epidemic. He had read that there were so many dead bodies piled up in Bombay and there was no place for them in the cemeteries.

On the fourth of February the British government promulgated some new acts under which government officers were given special powers to deal with the epidemic. A plague committee was constituted with the British officer Rand as its president. The cruel, inhuman Rand under whose command another plague spread in the guise of the natural epidemic – a plague of oppressing the unfortunate and helpless public. The white soldiers would tramp through gardens, prayer rooms, kitchens with their heavy boots. They would go into people's homes forcibly, conducting searches. Under the pretext of destroying germs, they would burn clothes, bedding, string beds and other things, leaving behind flames and helpless sighs.

People abandoned their homes and the city. Intimidated by this horrific dance of death even government servants, uncaring of their jobs, locked up their homes hoping that they had kept the 'white epidemic' at bay. However, many of them were pulled down from buses and trains and forcibly sent to hospitals though they were not infected. And going to the hospital meant certain death. Even leaders fled from the city but Tilak refused to leave Poona. He opposed Rand when he saw that Rand was spreading death and fear. He visited homes to try and stop terror and oppression. He criticised Queen Victoria strongly despite being aware of the implications. He did not care because he felt the entire country was a prison. The question was merely one of moving from a large prison to a smaller one, that is Mandalay Central Jail. After a while there was an official announcement of the end of the plague but the fire burning in the minds of the people did not douse off. After four months Rand was shot dead.

But why had Tilak said that sorrow and misfortune make a man stronger and more self-reliant? Madhav started introspecting. What had he himself done when faced with sorrow? He had escaped; run away leaving everything behind – his country, family, home and job.

Madhav had regretted his escapism, but only long after he had run away. Perhaps he felt it for the first time after reading about Tilak's life struggle and about Maharshi Karve who had fought for widow remarriage and women education. Karve was insulted every day by his neighbours after he married a widow. People used to spit on him from their windows and roofs as he passed by. But he did not run away like Madhav. He did not abandon his home. Why was this word 'desertion' troubling Madhav so much after so many years?

Quickly climbing up the stairs of Singh Garh, Madhav moved ahead and then stopped suddenly and drew a deep breath. Tilak must have also stood here once taking deep breaths. The same air of Singh Garh would have filled his lungs as well, Madhav thought. Would he have felt like this all the time, twenty-five years ago?

As Madhav breathed out, the answer came to his mind, 'No'. At that time he would have dismissed these feelings as emotional, foolish patriotism. 'Patriotism' was merely an empty word for him when he still lived in his country. It was only when he went to live in America that he was filled with the desire to understand its true meaning. He had asked himself whether patriotism was merely remembering the corn and millet bread of home when one was living at alien soil. Was it just love for a pickle redolent or memories of one's mother? Was it just the flash of memory which reminded one of the sight of the moon from the roof of his village home? No, certainly not.

While in abroad Madhav tried to get to know his land, his roots. He read the history of India for the first time; acquainted himself with the struggle for Independence. He felt the same anguish within him which, he thought, his ancestors must have felt once upon a time. Though he was a Maharashtrian he had been reduced to tears when he read about the cruelties borne by his Bihari ancestors who were not even permitted to walk upright in their own streets due to the British oppression. They had to crawl on their bellies and walk on all fours like dogs whenever they left their homes. And if they ever forgot that, they were whipped. How long could they stay imprisoned in their homes?

He got to know Tilak, Karve, Gokhale, Phule – all belonging to his state – only after he had left it. Mahatma Gandhi had said that Poona was like a beehive of workers who were all dedicated to good deeds. He had studied something about them in school but merely enough to scrape through his exams. In America, when he re-acquainted himself with Indian history, Bal Gangadhar Tilak had become his hero. He had read that Tilak was very fond of the fort of Singh Garh and often used to go and stay there. That day he was standing in the same fort and he could feel the fragrance of Tilak's struggle in the air. The thought of Tilak immediately brought Burma's Mandalay Central Jail to Madhav's mind, as though he had seen Mandalay with his own eyes. Tilak was imprisoned there for six years in a tiny cell; six-seven arms-length long and four arms-length broad. What a fate for such a brave and intelligent man! In jail he was given pen and paper only once a month to write a letter to his family. Despite these circumstances, his mental faculties were such that he had managed to write an 800 page book – *Geeta Rahasya* – on a notebook with a tiny pencil in 108 days.

Madhav had understood and felt his own roots after living on American soil. Perhaps that was why when they had visited Shaniwarwada before coming to Singh Garh that day, he had read the official notice outside the fort and told Jyoti to take Siddhi around. He himself had remained outside. This had not happened before. He didn't feel like going in. The notice said the Peshwas had signed a treaty with the British against Tipu Sultan in that fort. It was only by such treachery that Tipu was finally defeated. As soon as he read Tipu Sultan's name on the inscription outside Shaniwarwada Madhav had remembered Edinborough.

Jyoti and Siddhi had entered Shaniwarwada after buying their tickets. Standing outside, Madhav was watching a replay of an old event in his mind. Siddhi was about six-seven years old when they had gone to Edinborough on a trip and seen Tipu Sultan's sword in a museum. The arms which wielded that sword must have been really strong and powerful, Madhav had thought. There was an inscription near the sword which said that it had belonged to an Indian warrior who had been defeated but who was a 'lion' in the true sense of the word. Jyoti had told Siddhi that Tipu Sultan was an Indian who was defeated by the British by deception and his sword was brought here. The little girl had innocently remarked, 'Now that we are here, why don't we take it back to India and leave it with granny?' Madhav had been moved by this innocent suggestion. Remembering this he could not even bear to stand in front of the main gate of Shaniwarwada and made his way to the Lal Mahal to see the statue of Jijabai.

Soon after they travelled to Singh Garh through the Swargate, Siddhi had startled him. 'Papa, what are you thinking? Let's go up.'

'Yes, yes...you people go ahead, I will follow.'

'Madhav, are you OK? What happened?' Jyoti and the driver had also caught up with him.

'Baby, go up quickly otherwise the sun will be too warm,' the driver said.

'Come on, Papa...' Then after a pause Siddhi said, 'OK, I will go up with Driver uncle. You come later. You are a big bore.' Siddhi moved ahead, followed by the smiling driver.

'Madhav . . .?' Jyoti tried to question him.

'Jyoti, please, why don't you also go along with them? I want to sit here for a while,' Madhav replied.

'But will you come up?'

'Yes, yes...give me five-ten minutes.'

'As you wish.' Jyoti started climbing up. Madhav sat down on some stones at the edge of the stairs. Memories were crowding his mind like the visible and invisible particles present in the air around him.

Madhav settled in America after getting a job in the Atlanta-based Center for Disease control – one of the largest agencies in the world conducting research against diseases. He had been stunned when he saw their labs. At that time there were no such research facilities in India. He had called Jyoti to Atlanta and cut off his connections with his Bangalore institution. But one of his colleagues, Prasad, used to send him mails once in a while and Madhav would reluctantly respond to it. Prasad sent him a detailed mail informing him that a research facility was created in Bangalore to store biological items and a lab was set up to conduct research on viruses. Prasad was overjoyed. He said that there were no pens or paper in the lab. Everything was done with the help of computers and machines. No object could be taken into the lab from outside and if it had to be taken in, it couldn't be brought out again because it could be contaminated. It was burnt and destroyed if it was no longer required. Only human beings could go in and come out. When any scientist or his assistant went in, he first had to leave all his clothes and belongings in a locker and then step into a cabin next door where a shower of water fell on him. This happened three times. First he was showered with plain water, then with soapy water and finally with mineral water. Then he had to wear a space-suit like garment and cover himself completely before stepping into the lab. On his return he had to go through the same process again before changing into his ordinary clothes and walking out. The door of the shower cabin was automatic. Once someone stepped in, he couldn't emerge before the three showers were over. And when it opened the person could only move ahead, he couldn't come back as the system was entirely machine-controlled. Prasad was totally fascinated. After giving the entire description of the Bangalore lab, he wanted to know from Madhav whether the Atlanta lab had a similar system or even better.

After a few days Prasad informed him that the director had given him the charge of the lab. So much responsibility had oiled the wheels of Prasad's life; had given it a meaning. Thereafter he became so busy that his communication with Madhav almost came to a halt and Madhav himself was so busy that he had no time to wonder about Prasad's silence.

Then after a while there was a long email from Prasad. It seemed there had been an incident. One holiday, when the lab was being cleaned, Prasad went there with his director Mukhopadhyaya to discuss some matter concerning the facility. But first he wanted to discuss something about the shower room with him. Prasad opened the door of the locker room with his electronic card. He walked in first and then opened the door to the shower room. Mukhopadhyaya was just behind him. When Prasad opened the door to the shower room the director entered first followed by Prasad. Prasad held onto the door of the shower room. The door stayed open and the showers did not function. As they were discussing the problem Prasad unconsciously lifted his hand from the door. 'Oh my god! What will happen now?' he said, but the door had closed.

Mukhopadhyaya laughed, 'What will happen! We will have to bathe with our clothes on and go home in wet clothes.'

'But together?' Prasad said.

'Why are you scared? We are wearing our clothes, aren't we?'

'But we will have to leave them here before entering the next room.' Both of them had burst out laughing. Then suddenly Prasad looked perturbed, 'But why hasn't the shower started yet?' His face was becoming pale.

Even Mukhopadhyaya was alerted, 'Yes...why hasn't it started?'

'Damn it! Maybe the tanks are empty because of the cleaning.' When Prasad said this Mukhopadhyaya was flabbergasted, 'What does that mean?'

'It means that the door will not open unless the three showers are over, and we don't know when the tanks will be filled up.'

'Oh no!' Mukhopadhyaya said in his hoarse voice. Then he noticed that Prasad was sweating heavily. His shirt was wet and sweat beaded his forehead. Prasad was pressing his chest with both his hands. Mukhopadhyaya was beginning to feel scared. 'Prasad... Prasad...'

'There is no emergency switch or alarm here. Are we going to die like this... no!' Mukhopadhyaya was alarmed when he heard this. He didn't say anything and just sat down with a thud on the floor and sat there quietly for a while. Prasad had also sat down because he couldn't control his body and his accelerated heart beat. Mukhopadhyaya looked at him. Then he took off his shoes, put them under his head, and lay down.

'Sure, you can sleep... make a pillow and sleep. It doesn't matter even if you die. Your children are grown up. They are settled but...' Prasad's anxiety was making him agitated. When Mukhopadhyaya remained silent he started crying, 'I don't want to die now... all my work is unfinished. What will happen to my wife and children? I don't want to die!'

Mukhopadhyaya was looking at Prasad. He was silent but his mind was working rapidly. Prasad is a heart patient and he is panicking. What if something happens to him? How long can the oxygen in this small room suffice for two people? Suppose the shower doesn't work till evening... then? Mukhopadhyaya thought to himself.

Prasad dragged himself to the door and started beating it. 'Open! Open the door! Someone open it... I don't want to die now,' Prasad was crying out aloud.

'Prasad, you know this room is soundproof. The door will not open, and no one can open it from outside... you know that. Prasad... listen.'

'No, I don't want to die... and you are relaxing at such time... do something.'

'We can't do anything,' Mukhopadhyaya said and then kept silent. But Prasad's shirt had become completely wet even without the shower. His face was drenched with tears and sweat. He was constantly mumbling something and Mukhopadhyaya was looking at him silently. For a few moments the situation remained the same – one person in panic and the other silent. Then suddenly the shower started working. Perhaps the tank had been filled with water.

Memories also have knots, who knew which knot it was about to unravel that day? A sliver of feeble sunshine touched Madhav's face as he sat on the stony steps of Singh Garh. He was sitting quietly in the sunshine.

How had Prasad and Mukhopadhyaya felt at the moment when they were confronting death? Both had reacted differently. Prasad was shouting, but was Mukhopadhyaya really as composed as he seemed to be? We are so afraid of death, he thought. Hadn't he run away to America just to escape this fear, the acknowledgement of death?

After recovering from the incident Prasad had written that perhaps they were trying to run before they could learn to walk in his country; conducting experiments for which they were not yet ready. Then he had asked whether any similar incident had happened in the research lab in Atlanta and if there was any possibility of such thing ever happening.

Madhav had thought a lot about these questions for a few days and had finally concluded that the incident had merely been a random event. He didn't feel like sending a reply to Prasad. How could he tell him that in the labs there, under the pretext of finding cures for different illnesses, research was also done to discover viruses to wipe out the human race if the world was ever on the brink of a third world war! Research was conducted to determine which viruses could destroy human beings in greater numbers and then attempts were made to create them.

Madhav often thought that the scientists who participated in such experiments were also human, so what happened to them once they went into their labs wearing their lab suits? Do they leave their humanity and souls behind in the lockers along with their clothes? How does it feel to leave behind your soul and humanity every morning as you go in, and collect it again in the evenings?

But this cruelty towards the human race and inhumanity was not exclusive to the modern age. He remembered the time, nearly 250 years ago, when the commander-in-chief of the British army, Lord Jeffery Amherst, had written a letter to his friend suggesting – 'Couldn't we somehow pass on the small-pox germs to these Red Indians through their blankets? We have to make every possible effort to reduce their numbers.' This was the time when Britain and America were fighting with France and its allies – the Red Indians – for the possession of the land which later came to be known as Canada. The Red Indians were given blankets contaminated with the small-pox virus and a large number of them died of the disease. The disease spread like wildfire and swallowed half the population. Perhaps Britain was the first country to introduce the idea of germ warfare and use a 'small-pox epidemic' as a weapon of war.

What is this world? What are we? The same fights, the same struggles, in every civilisation for centuries. Depriving man of his human rights and that too in a cruel, soul-shattering manner. Why? For what reason? The answer may lie in the old principle of physics about light.

Any object, sight or happening only becomes visible to us when the light which is reflected off it reaches us. That means along with the light the speed at which it travels also determines when we see the object, event or happening. If the reflected light reaches us after a hundred years we see the event only after a hundred years.

However, that day Madhav found himself bathed in a light which was merely eight years old. At that time he was still in Bangalore. There was an outbreak of brain fever in a small village called Bellary near Mysore which was killing young children. The number of the dead was increasing every day. This disease often occurred in that area but had never been so virulent. Doctors concluded that it was brain fever again but after a while, when the blood samples of the children were examined, very few of them tested positive for brain fever. By now the government had declared that Bellary was afflicted with brain fever which was killing children in large numbers. Some doctors protested in a muted manner, questioning how the outbreak could be termed 'brain fever' when all the blood samples didn't test positive for it. Keshav Mahadevan had completely dedicated himself to researching the disease. He had lost track of everything else in his life, almost to the point of madness.

Madhav remembered that at that time Keshav's daughter Antara had such high fever that he, Jyoti and Keshav's wife had taken her to a nursing home. Keshav seemed to have cut himself off even from his own self. When the attendant brought his dinner from home he would find Keshav's lunch still untouched. Keshav's wife would phone Madhav and he would force Keshav to stop work for a while and eat. Only Madhav could do this because he was the one who was holding steady the narrow ladder of dreams which Keshav was climbing gingerly.

After exhaustive research Keshav discovered that the disease wasn't brain fever but a new virus. Because this virus was a new discovery in the field of medical research and had first afflicted Bellary, it was named after the village. Keshav passed on the message, through official channels, to the health ministry that the outbreak was a new virus called 'Bellary'. However, the hands of the democratic government were tied. It had already publicised that it was an outbreak of 'brain fever' and that the government had done everything possible to contain it. Now it seemed degrading to go back on its earlier claims and devalue its efforts at controlling the outbreak. Or perhaps the government had no faith in the efficiency of its own medical researcher. So the government did not acknowledge the discovery of the new virus. Keshav was also given strict instructions, by the powers that be, not to mention his discovery in public. He was prohibited from publishing any paper on the topic for a year. Perhaps the government needed some time!

Keshav's paper on the 'Bellary' virus was ready. For him each moment of that year passed like a decade. Then, one day, there was an article in a foreign newspaper about a foreign agency which had conducted tests on the blood samples of children in Bellary and had concluded that the claim of the Indian government declaring the outbreak as brain fever, was wrong. The agency stated that it was a new virus and took the entire credit for the discovery. Keshav found that the foreign agency had conducted the same experiments and used the same techniques which he had applied. They had discovered the same virus and got credit for its discovery. Keshav's paper had been shoved into some dark corner of an almirah – abandoned and neglected. And Keshav's dream? It was languishing somewhere in the dark, lost in the chasms of failure, disbelief, regret and helplessness. Alone and silent!

This news which reached people through the daily newspaper in the morning had already been heard by Keshav late at night on foreign news channels. He ate his dinner silently after being urged by his wife and went out for a short walk. And he never returned. Never.

He went straight to his office within the campus and spent some time there, alone. He even surfed the internet. God knows what he looked at! Then he linked his American web camera to the internet. He tied a strong rope to the ceiling fan at some distance from the camera, made a noose and placed a chair under it. Nobody knew where had he got that rope from! He climbed onto the chair, put the noose around his neck and stood still for a few seconds. Suddenly he kicked the chair away and hung himself from the noose.

The web-cam had recorded all this and projected it to the rest of the world through the internet. Keshav was no more. He had committed suicide. He had scribbled a few shaky words on his table – 'my dreams are no more'.

In the morning there was uproar across the world, the country, Bangalore and in Keshav's institution, but within Madhav something had come to a halt. Each frame, each scene recorded by the web-cam had frozen his being like cubes of ice. Keshav's face was so peaceful at that moment. But his mind? The cubes followed Madhav wherever he went during the day, the night, in his sleep and his dreams. He decided that he wouldn't stay there any longer. He got an offer the next week and immediately left for Atlanta.

'Papa, we have even come back and you are still sitting here.' Siddhi was out of breath. She must have run back. Jyoti and the driver still hadn't returned. Madhav merely smiled. Siddhi had come back but perhaps he hadn't yet found *his* way back.

'Anyway, tell me, what time will you go to fetch Antara didi in the evening?'

'Yes, in the evening...' Madhav was gathering himself together.

'Yes, but at what time?'

'You tell me...seven o'clock?' Madhav asked.

'That will be too late. Please bring her earlier...I want to meet her. I have lots of things to talk about with her.'

'All right, I will give her a call. Five o'clock is OK?'

'OK.'

When Madhav talked to Prasad on coming to Poona he got to know that Keshav's daughter Antara was now twenty-two years old and was doing her M.A. from Pune University. Memories of Keshav always used to haunt Madhav whenever he came back to India. This time when he heard Antara was in Pune his fingers automatically dialed her number given to him by Prasad. The voice of a twenty-two-year-old girl had responded to his call, but in his mind he could still recall the innocent face of a seven-year-old solitary girl wearing a frock and ribbons. Her lonely, innocent eyes that had asked, 'Where is my Papa?'

He had invited Antara to dinner at home that night and he had to go and pick her up.

'What gift will you give her?' Siddhi asked.

'Whom do we have to give a gift?' Jyoti asked, as she came closer.

Siddhi replied enthusiastically, 'To Antara didi. Aren't we going to give her something?' Jyoti just smiled. When she got no answer, she caught hold of Madhav's arm and asked again, 'Tell me, Papa, what will we give her?'

Madhav stood up. As he dusted his trousers, he said, 'Whatever your mother says, sweetheart,' and started climbing down the stairs before everyone. He walked so fast that Jyoti and Siddhi's voices became fainter. Dashing to the bottom of the stairs he came to a sudden halt. Why was he running? Who was he running from? When he could find no answer he walked ahead slowly and sat down on the boundary wall of the fort which bordered the steps. He remembered a folk tale which was poised between myth and reality even till that day. After hundreds of years! It was a German folk-tale he had read in his native language and which he had thought about when he visited the place Hamlyn where it was based. The story was – 'The Pied Piper of Hamlyn'.

Siddhi was very small, perhaps just three years old, when they had gone on a trip to Germany. When they visited Hamlyn he found that the town still resonated with references to the folk story. It was reliving the myth at every instant. The people in the town claimed that the incident on which the story was based occurred in the thirteenth century when the town was overrun by rats. Because of those rats the city was often afflicted by plague but the people and the town administration could not find any solution to the problem. One day a stranger wearing motley clothes came into the town. He pulled a flute out of his pocket and started playing a beautiful tune. On hearing the music, all the rats came out of the stores, houses, drains and started following him. The entire town was stunned by the sight. The piper walked ahead, followed by hordes of rats dancing merrily to his tune. The road was thronged by rats. The Pied Piper kept walking till he reached the river. Then, instead of stopping, he walked into the water followed by the rats. When the water reached his shoulders he looked back playing on his pipe. All the rats had followed him into the river and drowned. The residents of Hamlyn stood on the river banks watching the Pied Piper in amazement and disbelief.

Why did this piper, who could rid a town of rats with his music, appear only in Hamlyn? Why not here? Don't we need him as well? We are also threatened by the plague... there are rats here as well, Madhav thought. And why does the Pied Piper only take away rats? Why not mosquitoes and flies? Why not viruses? Viruses don't only cause physical illnesses. What do we call the viruses which infect our systems? Madhav felt that Keshav had not committed suicide, he had been consumed by a virus. But when it devoured Keshav, did it only consume him? What about the other scientists who were involved in the research with Keshav? Who destroyed the happiness of Keshav's wife and his daughter Antara? Wasn't it a virus? And now it seemed that a virus was slowly spreading through his own brain. Will there ever be a Pied Piper who will come and draw out all these viruses? Madhav had no answers to all these questions.

When he saw Jyoti and Siddhi coming along behind the driver, he stood up and walked towards the car. He felt as though Siddhi was once again asking him, 'What gift are we going to give to Antara didi?' He wished he could find a Pied Piper for Antara; one who could draw away all such viruses one by one from every country in the world, once and forever.

When the Piper would look back once the water reached his shoulders, they would all be dead just like the rats of plague. But even before destroying the viruses the Piper should destroy those selfish people who allow such viruses to grow. They don't destroy them well in time and thus spreads an illness which takes on a frightening shape as it crosses the borders of cities, countries and languages, Madhav was still thinking. Taking on the shape not merely of an epidemic but of a pandemic. Does this virus spread on its own throughout the world, or does someone spread it? Is this what is meant by the word 'global'? Madhav thought of Siddhi's globe which was balanced on a spike. He saw a silhouette of Keshav on the globe and murmured, 'pandemic'.